Alexander Ruth

Merry Xmas

24 + 1
Christmas Tales

Butterfly Adventures in
Santa's Secret City

Martha   Johnny

Sonja   Dago

Santa

Printed in Germany by Amazon Distribution GmbH, Leipzig

Copyright© August 2013 Alexander Ruth, 1st Edition

Illustrations: copyright© Lucas Schmidhofer and Sabine Birgels

The moral right of the author has been asserted.

ISBN-13: 978-1491271810

ISBN-10: 1491271817

A catalogue record for this publication is available from the Deutsche Nationalbibliothek; further information on this title: http://dnb.d-nb.de.

Translated by Maxine White

Once upon a time, not long before Christmas, winter fell upon the land and thoughts turned to peace all over the world.

Snowflakes sought their way from above the rooftops to Santa's Secret City at the North Pole, as did the brave butterflies Darfo, Martha, Sonya and Johnny, along with their companions, the three electric blue fireflies and the fearful phoenix. They had one mission: to make Christmas bigger, better and more perfect!

The butterflies are daily visitors to begin with, but soon become Santa's Official Little Helpers and are allowed to move into living quarters at Santa's Secret City.

These 24 + 1 stories tell of the little rascals' adventures as they seek out their old friend Santa again this year. Some are short, some are long – simply glide into a fairy tale world.

Of course there's no question that the stories are true.

Here's how it all began…

1

Operation Wish List

The snow fell softly on Santa's Secret City at the North Pole. The houses looked like they'd been dusted with a coat of icing sugar. All was peaceful and quiet, but for a very faint sound:

"Pssssst, *careful*, be really careful!" whispered Darfo Butterfly to Martha, who was balancing on a *huge* pile of paper, wobbling as she tried to add more pages. The little rascal peered around the pile cautiously. Golden light poured from the open door at the end of the corridor.

HE was sitting at his desk going through his lists. They could clearly hear him sighing and scratching his head. Scrat, scrat, scrat.

"Ready?"

Martha Butterfly nodded vigorously and scrambled down, all of a tizzy. She had such butterflies in her tummy!

The smell of mince pies and sherry was wafting into the store room from the magical office.

"It's high time we got out of here, otherwise he'll be thinking there's no end to all our back orders!"

"Okay," whispered little Martha in almost a giggle. Without daring to take their eyes off the office door, the Wish List Team crept backwards carefully, *sooooo* carefully, to the secret, hidden door at the back of the room up here at the North Pole.

There was nothing quite like carrots for keeping Dasher, Dancer, Prancer, Vixen, Comet, Cupid, Donner and Blitzen occupied. "Chomp, chomp, chomp!" was all they could hear from the barn as they sneaked past.

They crept out into the wintry air. Their fireflies were waiting for them, glowing electric blue, and their friend the phoenix circled watchfully in the sky. Johnny the Macho Butterfly and Sonya the Butterfly Warrior had been keeping a lookout. They'd done it! The little rascals heaved a great sigh of relief. Now dozens more children would be getting their Christmas presents. Gosh, the things they got up to, just so that children all over the world could have their dearest wishes granted!

2

The Wish List Inspector

The snow fell softly on Santa's Secret City at the North Pole. Smoking chimneys were the only sign of life. Everyone was hard at work, including the old man. A gold-glowing finger swept down the list.

"Luna, aged 4, Meerbusch, Germany – rocking horse," he read. The man in the red suit peered across at the Naughty Book. No mention of Luna.

"Good girl!" he boomed in a deep voice and smiled. Then he moved on.

"Ben, aged 5, Stuttgart, Germany – bunk bed slide." A quick look to the right. Not listed.

"Very good."

The little helpers sat next to him as he worked, swinging their legs and chomping candy floss. They were so nervous and excited that it was only with great effort that they managed not to talk. They were not allowed to speak unless spoken to when Santa was going through his lists. He needed every bit of concentration he could muster up. Of course things would be back to normal again once he'd finished. The butterflies, the little rascals, were here on official duty, the same as every year.

Then to the next entry on the list:

"Jonah, aged 7, Hamburg – new bike." He'd outgrown his old one.

"Hmmm," Santa stroked through his long, white beard and beckoned to Darfo. He lifted up his sunglasses, (which everyone wore when he was going through his lists because the magical glow was so bright. It was the same magical glow that he used to send the good children's wishes to the toy factory, to be made into presents by the elves) then he squinted at the list and nudged the butterfly. "Do you know this lad?"

Darfo raised his sunglasses slightly and looked at the list. He couldn't read, but that didn't matter as there was a photograph of the boy next to the entry. Jonah was holding a stick of candy floss in his hand, which might have been a bit of a giveaway, but Santa was none the wiser.

"Oooh, of course I do, that's Jonah! Great boy, lovely lad!"

Santa Choccy (that's what the butterflies sometimes called him, just for fun) looked at him suspiciously. Darfo slapped his sunglasses back on, grinned widely and gave Santa the thumbs up. "He's a great boy, honestly, no trouble at all."

"Why do I get the feeling I've already seen this wish list before?" asked Santa, raising his eyebrows without looking up at the butterflies – his gaze was fixed on his list.

"Nooooo, that isn't possible," replied a chorus of Martha, Darfo, Johnny and Sonya.

Whatever gave him that idea? Tee-hee-hee...

3

Secret Snacks

The snow fell softly on Santa's Secret City at the North Pole. The snowflakes allowed themselves to be carried by the light breeze until they found a nice place to settle.

Secretly, ever-so secretly, the fluttersome secret agents crept into Santa's bedroom.

"Zzzzzzzzzzzzzz!" snored Santa.

"Hee, hee, hee!"

"Ssshhhh!!!"

The electric blue fireflies held their hands over their mouths to stifle their nervous giggles.

Darfo and Johnny rushed to the foot end of the bed. Martha and Sonya slid the bar of chocolate right up close to Santa. He didn't wake up.

"Zzzzzzzzzzzzzz!" he carried on snoring loudly. Of course he needed his sleep because he'd soon have lots of work to do.

"Hurry up!" Johnny hissed to Darfo.

"I am doing, I am doing!" Darfo snapped back. Johnny lifted up the covers and Darfo took a feather out of his leather pouch. Santa wiggled his toes.

"Oooh!" Martha exclaimed loudly, quite by accident! With a big snore and a snort, their victim turned over: *goodness, gracious, great butterflies of fire!*

One big PUFF and the phoenix changed back to ashes in fright. But the old man just wiggled his bum and turned back over.

"PHEWWW!" they all breathed out. With a bright flash, the phoenix burst back to life from the ashes and positioned himself by the door as lookout. Then it was *three, two, one,* TICKLE TIME! Darfo set about Santa's feet with the feather. It didn't take long before Santa was laughing in his sleep and a crackling, golden glow ran up and down his body: Santa's magic!

This is just what the bunch of rascals were aiming at, because as soon as the magic glow touched the bar of chocolate, the chocolate burst into a hundred-million-trillion-squillion-zillion pieces just like popcorn, "Pop-pop-pop… Pop-pop… Pop-pop-pop-pop-POP!" and there was chocolate everywhere.

"Hooray!" they rejoiced (in a whisper), waving their arms around wildly to catch as many pieces as they could.

Darfo dropped the feather, they all grabbed as much as they could carry and vanished out into the night.

My-oh-my! At this time of year they worked from dawn till dusk helping Santa, and that made getting hold of a decent snack at the North Pole *very* complicated!

4

The Official Sleigh Crew

The snow fell softly and endlessly. The magical office was filled with the smell of freshly baked biscuits. Candlelight flickered, fending off the darkness. The butterflies sat on the little table in front of Father Christmas. Their legs dangled over the edge. The time had come.

Luckily for the butterflies, they had lost all concept of how much work was yet to be done. Wish lists were pouring in from all parts of the globe.

The phoenix was trying to catch the electric blue fireflies, who couldn't help but laugh at him. Santa still had his back to the butterflies. Then he turned around on his old, wooden swivel chair: *CREEEEAK!*

There they sat, beaming from ear to ear. He breathed out heavily.

The elves marched in. They took position behind the most important man of the year.

"Hee, hee, hee!"

Martha couldn't help herself. They ALL knew what was coming next!

One of the elves went to the front and gave Santa the latest wish list update. Santa let out a little sigh. "Hmmmm," he stroked through his white beard absent-mindedly and peered at the little rascals. They were all wrapped up warm and ready to go.

"And you're sure the high number of wish lists this year has nothing to do with you?"

Shocked, they shook their heads silently. Whatever made him think that? Why, that was almost an accusation!

"Urghhhh," he got up slowly. Then he made the routine gesture for them to all get up too.

CLATTER, CLATTER, CLATTER, they all jumped to their feet, grinning from ear to ear.

"Well then, here we go!"

A golden ring of magic crackled up and down
Santa's body from the bottom of his boots, round
his tummy, up his back, along his nose and across
his eyes to the top of his head. When it reached
the top, the ring of magic clapped together and
then split into two, shooting down his arms.
Sparks went down his index fingers, which he
pointed at Martha, Darfo, Sonya and Johnny.
The phoenix and the fireflies hovered mid-air.
The faces of the little rascals set into a silly grin.
PLOP, PLOP, PLOP, PLOP!
Four wet golden spheres hit the squad and
covered them from head to toe.
SPLAT, SPLAT, SPLAT, SPLAT!
Another layer of magic covered them all, soaking
into their skin.
"Hee, hee, hee," the butterflies giggled, rubbing in
the gold.
They could see their veins turn from blue to gold
as the magic pumped around their bodies. Then
there was one more big flash. Rays shot in all
directions, dazzling them before being absorbed
into their bodies. Then a gentle, pulsating rush. It
was done.

14

"Yippeeeeeeee!"

Martha, Darfo, Sonya and Johnny leapt up and hugged one another. Not only were they Santa's Little Helpers, they were now also the Official Sleigh Crew: the Christmas Butterflies who were allowed to fly with Santa Claus! And they were even granted living quarters – their very own Butterfly House in Santa's Secret City!

There was so much going on at the North Pole, but of course that had nothing at all to do with the butterflies, honest...

5

Surprise Practice

Loads of snow fell at the North Pole. The darkness was only broken by the lights of Santa's Secret City.

All of a sudden, the sirens went off, "*Eeee-oooh, Eeee-oooh, Eeee-oooh!*" emergency alert!

The noise instantly woke Martha, Darfo, Johnny and Sonya. They leapt out of their four-storey bunk bed, dashed up the spiral staircase in the centre of the room and jumped onto the fireman's pole. They spun down to the ground and waited in expectation. They were ready.

"Quick, quick, quick!" called the elves, beckoning to them.

They followed the elves resolutely. What was going on?

They went past Santa's door on their way, but he wasn't in his office. "*Buzzzzzz!*" the three electric blue fireflies flew up and the phoenix appeared out of nowhere with a big *PUFF*. The elves just kept on walking and walking, but the butterflies had soon sussed out exactly where they were going.

"But... but... but..." stammered Johnny the Macho Butterfly. "It's not Christmas yet!"

Before they knew it, they were stood in front of a packed sleigh. Dasher, Dancer, Prancer, Vixen, Comet, Cupid, Donner and Blitzen were all harnessed up and grinning at the little rascals. The sleigh was packed sky-high with presents, but no sign of Santa anywhere.

"Quick, quick, quick!" the elves banged on the side of the sleigh. "You need to set off straight away! There was a mistake with the calendar! It's Christmas Eve today!"

The little rascals dived into place in a state of shock – they must save Christmas! They didn't doubt for a moment that there had been a mistake. These things happen. It could just as easily have happened to them.

"What are we supposed to do?"

"Here!" One of the elves gave Darfo the reins.

"The more you shake them, the faster they go. If you pull them gently, they think it's time for carrots and stop automatically."

Aha. Darfo nodded. He'd got it. It was easy.

"And this," said one of the elves, pointing to the red and green button with the heart on it, "is the hover button. Never switch it off when you're airborne!"

'Otherwise you'll end up with a Christmas disaster like in 2003…' whispered another elf to his neighbour.

"Ho-ho! Or like in 1998, 2001, 1999, 2008, 1963, 1985, 1978..." the list was endless!

Martha looked down anxiously.

"Don't worry – just don't press the button when you're in the air!"

17

The little rascals nodded, awe-stricken.

"And here's the list!"

"But there are 153,146 million addresses!"

"Don't worry, you'll have them done in ten minutes!"

The elf gave Donner a sharp slap on its hind quarters and *whoooosh* off they went. *Clip-clop, clip-clop, clip-clop*, Martha, Darfo, Johnny and Sonya were thrown back in their seats as the first hazard came into sight: they were racing straight towards the toy factory wall!

Just in time, Johnny slapped the button with the palm of his hand and *wheeeeee* they shot up into the dark night sky.

The elves stood and grinned at the fireflies and the phoenix, who were left behind.

"Do you think they'll manage it?"

"Never!"

"Then *UNFORTUNATELY* we'll have to tell the old guy – and there's only one logical conclusion he can come to after that kind of failure!"

"Yep!"

"Yep!"

"Yep!" the elves cried out, one after the other, until they heard heavy footsteps stomping through the snow.

At that point, the sleigh was whizzing round the earth above their heads for the fourth time. The elves secretly pressed a remote control button.

A message came out of the slit in front of Darfo: "Can you please press down the red button hard." Written in pictures, of course. He understood the "please" straight away.

"Of course I can," he said out loud and pressed down the button, much to Darfo, Sonja and Martha's dismay. The result was visible down below.

"What's going on up there?" growled Santa, as the first present fell from the sky and landed right on his nose. He gawped at it in disbelief.

"Test run." The elves pointed upwards. The sleigh was doing a nosedive from the sky, heading straight for Father Christmas.

"Oh my goodness!" he gasped.

"There are just far too many butterflies for one sleigh!" whispered the elves to Santa.

"Mmmm, yes, you're probably right," he muttered, scratching his head under his red hat. Fortunately, Johnny managed to gather his bearings just in time and pressed the heart button as the sleigh was barely 20 metres off the ground. The sleigh stopped its dramatic descent and glided gently to the ground, coming to a halt a short distance away from Santa and the elves. As soon as the cloud of snow dust had dispersed, Santa walked up to Martha, Darfo, Johnny and Sonya, huffing and puffing.

"What the heavens is going on here?"

The butterflies stared at him, lost for words. Martha's face was a pale shade of green and Darfo's hands were still shaking.

"Too many butterflies in one sleigh," said the elves again, and the little rascals just echoed them: *"Too many butterflies in one sleigh!"*

"Too many butterflies in one sleigh" was still going through Santa's mind as one of the elves began to explain:

"Due to the ergomatricular properties of the sleigh, with its cybernautical star-seeking mode set to accommodate the exact body mass of Father

Christmas, it's highly likely that the butterflies are just not suited to driving the sleigh, especially not all of them at once!"

Santa looked at the elves, mimicking surprise, patting his big, round tummy.

"Are you trying to tell me I'm FAT?"

"No sir... not at all... never... only the sleigh has been pre-set for your weight!"

"So now what?"

"Well if we were to..." the elves waved to the others, who marched off all at once.

"Whooo-ahhh!" they cried, followed by the ringing of bells – lots of little bells. And suddenly, there stood four sleighs. A blue one, a red one, a green one... and a pink one. They were all drawn by young reindeer, who were desperate to be up in the air for first time this Christmas.

"Wowwww!" the butterflies gasped.

"We expected there to be some problems, so we prepared THESE."

Father Christmas looked at the elves suspiciously, but they were all highly professional and kept straight faces. Then he looked across at the butterflies. It was plainly obvious that they had nothing to do with any of this.

"Too many butterflies in one sleigh," muttered Father Christmas. He lifted his belly up and let go with a big wobble. Then he waved them off.

"Oh, do whatever you like, as long as you don't spoil Christmas."

Shivering from the cold, he headed for the warm indoors, leaving them all standing there.

Darfo, Martha, Johnny and Sonya still couldn't quite believe it. Mouths wide open, they stared at *their* reindeer and *their* sleighs.

You see, there are always some who are willing to do more for others than for themselves, although we don't always notice…

6

Naughty Knave Rupert's Sack of Coal

The sea was calm and still and the snow fell softly on Santa's Secret City at the North Pole. Suddenly, the silence was broken.

"You!" the butterfly girl ordered angrily. "Come here!"

Chests stuck out, the butterflies were marching up and down in their official capacity as Santa's Little Helpers. Martha's finger was pointing at somebody in a brown coat at the back. She beckoned to him. Father Christmas had popped to the shops with Mrs Claus. The butterflies were on their toy factory lunch break, so this gave them the ideal opportunity to do some more good for the children of the world.

"Show us what's in your sack!"

She was addressing Naughty Knave Rupert. Grumpily, he grabbed his sack: you know, the one that should be full of lumps of coal for naughty children. But not a sign of coal was to be seen! In his sack, would you believe it, were a leather belt, a fly swat and a baseball bat! He took them out of the sack and showed them to the little rascals.

Santa had sent him an invitation to a "quality control security check", on posh paper with a big wax seal on it. Big-Old-Boss-Santa always did random checks to make sure everything was going according to plan. Rupert was a bit surprised to see that his invitation was signed with four splattered, little handprints. But he imagined Santa must have his reasons for employing the mystical butterflies, Martha, Darfo, Johnny and Sonya. No doubt to help improve the Festival of Love.

Martha was really getting into her new role.

"Right! And now show me the other things you're still hiding!"

"Huh?" mumbled Rupert, pretending not to understand what she meant.

"Herumph... I can see QUITE clearly that you're hiding ALL SORTS in that bearskin coat of yours!" *If a job was worth doing, then it was worth doing well.*

"Drat!" snarled Rupert, making both Darfo and Sonya giggle.

In a flash, Rupert produced quite a collection of punishment tools – an electric shocker, hand cuffs, tear gas and a hammer!

That's it, he gestured, pretty annoyed, because that actually was it.

"Hey, can he not talk?" Darfo asked.

"Well, not any sense... in fact he talks such a load of rubbish that *he* should be the one being punished!"

"Hee, hee, hee!"

But the game was still on, as Martha had discovered something else.

"AHAA! And what's that sticking out of your boot under your trousers?"

"Umph," groaned Rupert. She really did see everything.

"Tusk-tusk!"

A quick, sweeping movement and, hey presto! She whisked out a giant, poisonous rattle snake and two tarantulas – which he actually always had with him, in case he had to punish someone really, really naughty.

"Hee, hee, hee!" giggled Sonya, Darfo and Johnny, taking a few paces back, out of range of the dangerous weapons.

"RIGHT!" Martha inflated her wings until they made her look *much* bigger. She'd really shown *him*!

"But now how's he supposed to punish the bad children?"

"Mmmm." Martha Butterfly scratched her head.

25

"Okay," she said, pointing at the fly swat. "You can keep that. For the *really* naughty ones."

A Quick Christmas Tip

"…Then you exchange your little sock on the mantelpiece for one of mummy's stockings," the butterflies told the little ones. "So there's much more room for presents!"

7

How to Process Wish Lists

The snow fell softly on Santa's Secret City at the North Pole. Frost decorated the window panes in flowery patterns and candlelight flickered in the windows of some of the buildings, where people had already started work.

Clunk, went the stamp. *Clunk!*

Stamp it and pass it on… The butterfly grabbed it and dashed off.

Clunk!

Next stamp. Pass it on. The next butterfly grabbed it and dashed off.

Clunk!

Next stamp. Pass it on again…

- Sudden pause –

"Huh?" Santa turned around inquisitively.

"Sorry!" Johnny mumbled between cheeks full of candy floss, grabbing the wish list and dashing off at double speed.

Clunk!

And the stamp - *missed*.

"Just a minute," said Santa. He scratched his forehead, deep in thought. "Can you bring back those last two wish lists?"

Gulp! Darfo and Johnny went chalky white.

"Ermmm… of course."

Sloooooowly, verrrrrrry sloooooowly, they went back and collected the last two sheets.

"Can you not get a move on? We need to be ready by December 24th!" his deep voice boomed. Father Christmas was only up to 'M' and they didn't have much time left.

They scurried back and handed over the requested wish lists. The phoenix flew by and swooped in to take a look, aflame with curiosity.

The most important man of the year compared the wish list in his hand to the other two.

"*Drat!*" hissed Darfo, but so quietly that Santa couldn't possibly hear.

He had given Johnny extra candy floss in exchange for neat handwriting. He only wanted to make sure that Martha got more presents! They'd even given Martha three names: Martha (her real name), Martha the Beautiful (Darfo's idea) and Martha the Princess (Johnny's idea). The address was the only thing that was the same on all three wish lists: 'Butterfly House'.

"Do three Marthas live in your house?" Santa looked up.

"Yuh, uh, absolutely" nodded the two boys.

Please, let him just put his 'OK' stamp on it and let us carry on! Darfo began to think about how wonderful it would be when Martha looked under the Christmas tree. He would be really popular then. And when girls are happy they get all emotional and hug and stuff… and if he just happened to be standing right next to her... *But all of that seemed in danger now.*

PUFF! The phoenix panicked and turned into a cloud of ash. Father Christmas squinted down at his Little Helpers. The butterfly boys stood there like innocent little lambs.

Dingelingeling!

The elves sounded the workshop bell as they suspected a production error.

"We're running out of time!"

"Hmmmm." Santa sighed heavily. "Alright, I suppose I'd better take your word for it."

CLUNK!

It was stamped!!! Darfo grabbed the wish lists and zipped around the corner grinning... and then squealed to a halt. He looked left and right, up and down – not a soul there – excellent! He took a boiled egg out of his jacket pocket and the stack of wish lists from up his jumper. Carefully he rolled the egg over the fresh, damp stamp and then rolled it onto each of the wish lists... wish lists from Martha the Lovely, Martha the Eternal, Martha the Star, Martha the One and Only, Martha the...

It'd be a sorry state of affairs if butterfly boys didn't manage to wangle themselves a few extra kisses at Christmas!

When Butterflies Kiss at Christmas

"When two butterflies kiss at Christmas, it magically makes Christmas much better for EVERYONE!" Martha whispered into Darfo's ear.

"*Reeeeeally?*"

"Yep!"

SNOGGGG!!!

8

The Girls' Gifts Workshop

The snow fell softly on Santa's Secret City at the North Pole. The odd silhouette flitted from door to door in the darkness. Indoors, the whole place was a hive of activity.

Butterfly boys Johnny and Darfo held their ears to the wooden door:

Bang, bang! Clunk, clunk! Hammer, hammer!

"This is where the girls' gifts are made!" Johnny playfully punched Darfo in the tummy.

"Ooouff!" Darfo exhaled.

The temperature soared as the fiery phoenix and the electric blue fireflies squeezed in between them. They wanted to know what was going on too!

It sounded something like *"Hee, hee, hee!"* and *"Ha, ha, ha!"*

"I bet they're sat there eating chocolate the whole time and drinking tea and making fun of us boys!" quipped Johnny the Macho Butterfly.

The others looked at him, astonished, stepping away from the door.

"*My* Martha is in there!" said Darfo, glaring at Johnny and tapping his forehead.

"She wouldn't do a thing like that!" *Especially not with them being here at the North Pole with Father Christmas and all that.*

Johnny thought about it for a moment and then agreed:

"You're right! It's far too cold for that up here!"

Darfo, the phoenix and the fireflies shook their heads in resignation. It was totally pointless trying to argue with him. But they were still curious to know what Martha and the girl elves were making. There was a heart-shaped decoration hanging from the door, and everyone knew that this was where the girls' presents were made.

"Why not take a look inside!" Johnny cried, pushing Darfo towards the door handle.

"Who, *me*?" Darfo leapt backwards. "You must be joking…"

Suddenly the door flew open and Martha stuck her head out.

"*HI* boys! You alright?"

32

"Martha!" Darfo smiled in delight, while two of the three fireflies tried to fly above Martha's head and catch a sneaky glimpse inside. She brushed them away subconsciously without so much as looking at them.

"Now you can tell that Johnny..."

"Hey, Martha, come back inside, there's work to be done!" called the girl elves, wanting to get on. With a charming smile and a wink, she turned to go back inside. Johnny swooned at her loveliness. *PLOPPP,* he fell to the floor!

"Is he talking rot again?" Martha asked Darfo.

Darfo nodded furiously and looked at the girls in anticipation.

"Well in that the case..." she said, calling to the girl elves: "Hey, do you think Darfo could have a quick look inside?"

"Yes, but make it quick! And be sure to use our trick afterwards!" replied one of the older girl elves, who was getting annoyed at the boys.

No sooner had she finished speaking as Darfo, the phoenix and the fireflies pushed their heads around the door. Mouths gaping wide, they could hardly believe what they saw.

33

"Ooooooh!"

"Aaaaaahhh!"

So that's what girls all around the world were getting for Christmas!

"Woweeee!!!"

Then Martha pushed in between them and shoved them out of the room.

"Right, you've seen enough! And don't let me catch you..."

"Hey, don't forget our little trick!" the girl elves called, and Martha giggled.

"Oh yes, silly me!"

She swiftly grabbed all the fireflies in one hand and the phoenix in the other, before he had chance to change into ashes. Stunned, they looked to Darfo for help, but it was too late.

Smacker, smacker, smacker, smacker!

She gave each of her victims a big, sloppy kiss on the lips...

Ooh la la! They all fainted in a big heap on the floor! Then she took Darfo's face in both hands and pulled his lips to hers.

Smackeroony!

"That was the best kiss in the universe," thought Darfo, all wobbly, weak at the knees and unable to get a word out. *"Gurgle, gurgle!"* was all he could manage, and thanks to the girls' little trick, he now wouldn't remember a thing about what he'd seen behind the door.

Of course it was a matter of honour that the girls didn't give anything away. Though it would've been nice to know what girls were getting for Christmas this year!

9

The Festival of Love

The darkness of night was broken by the perfect glow of golden, twinkling stars. Softly fell the snow.

Father Christmas was sat on the veranda after work, creaking to and fro in his rocking chair and enjoying a nice cup of hot honey with a hint of tea. The phoenix had settled down in Santa's beard, glowing warmly and listening to the fireflies' stories. Well, as long as they weren't too scary, because every time he became afraid, he burst into flames and singed Santa's beard!

Santa was nodding off. Dasher, Dancer, Prancer, Vixen, Comet, Cupid, Donner and Blitzen's muffled chit-chat could be heard in the background.

The only commotion came from Martha, Darfo, Sonya and Johnny's young reindeer, who were racing around in their pen. That didn't disturb the elves though, who were snoring away, their coats hanging up outside their windows to air.

All was calm at the North Pole: it wasn't long now until Christmas.

No-one seemed to have noticed that the little rascals were missing, that is to say, no-one except Mrs Claus. She suddenly started, looked up and stopped knitting.

Sniff, sniff, sniff!

It was absolutely normal to smell mince pies and sherry in these parts, but what else was *that* that she could smell? Surely the Christmas bakery didn't open again until the morning?

She carefully laid her knitting to one side and looked out of the window.

The phoenix was putting out her husband's beard in a panic. He seemed to have dozed off and didn't notice a thing. The elves had apparently all gone to bed... which made her very suspicious! And where were Martha, Darfo, Johnny and Sonya?

She was starting to get concerned. She yanked on her winter boots and draped her husband's red coat around her shoulders. She could smell his eau de cologne on the white collar, mmmmh!

She marched through the snow past the reindeer, *crunch, crunch, crunch!* Then she saw Johnny's lead reindeer sneaking out of its pen, Martha's reindeer team making heart shapes in the snow with their hooves and Sonya's reindeer trying to preach to Darfo's little darlings about honour and morals. All quite normal really, except for that smell in the air.

Sniff, sniff, sniff!

She was drawn as by an invisible force in the direction of the bakery. She could already make out the silhouettes of individual butterflies. They were marching through the darkness into the bakery, with fully laden wheelbarrows.

"Now then, now then," she thought, tugging the red coat more tightly around her as she hurried on.

As she got a bit closer, she could hear the oven, flour mills and rolling pins in full action.

Clatter, crunch, boom, rattle, ping!

She had soon reached the bakery window and breathed warm air onto the frozen pane, rubbing a little hole in the ice with her hand… She could hardly believe her eyes! There they all stood, aprons on, baking biscuits. A motherly smile lit up her face as she made sense of things: they didn't have time to bake during the daytime!

Martha was stood at the absolutely-totally-extremely ancient leather-bound recipe book, entering new recipes with a wax crayon. Johnny and Sonya were baking them.

Mrs Claus sniffed with joy. Was she dreaming, or could this be real? She rubbed her eyes hard. Oh my, the ingredients would make Christmas magical for everyone for ever and ever! And they were baking up a big supply, too!

38

Wow, she could hardly believe her eyes. She was filled with gratitude. It was really happening, it was true.

But… but… surely it was impossible – *though apparently not*. The little rascals had flown up to the stars and had asked them for some more star dust. Magic dust. The dust that cherubs use to bring two people together. One pinch of it was sufficient to last a lifetime. It bound hearts together, taking away hate, anger and quarrelling and replacing them with love and forgiveness.

"Oooh!" sighed Mrs Claus. "What… what… what a very special gift!"

Only the butterflies could get dust from the stars… and… and… they were using this special ability to warm people's hearts forever.

The stardust biscuits would be delivered to people's homes: they'd be placed on tables, under Christmas trees and in bedrooms all over the world!

A tear of joy rolled down her cheek. She turned around quietly and crept back with a nice, warm feeling inside and a feeling of thankfulness towards the little creatures.

She finally reached the veranda and looked at the rocking chair. The phoenix was dozing amid a gentle glow in Santa's beard, alongside the electric blue fireflies. Her eyes welled up as she looked down at her husband. She leant down and gave him a gentle kiss.

"Thank you," she whispered to him, as her lips touched his cheek.

Now she understood why the butterflies were here on earth – and they had their very own interpretation of the Festival of Love...

10

The Chocolate Santa Factory

The sweet smell of candy floss, biscuits and sherry wafted around Santa's Secret City at the North Pole. The whole place was buzzing with activity. The elves dashed about frantically and the reindeer were galloping around a specially built snow test track. The phoenix and the electric blue fireflies were making ice sculptures by melting the ice and forming it into beautiful stars, deer and other figurines.

Father Christmas was stuck in his office mumbling and muttering as he worked his way through a mountainous pile of wish lists. Mrs Claus had taken charge of the Christmas bakery once more when suddenly, BANG!!!

A big explosion sounded out, shaking everyone and everything up. Coffee cups fell from the table, fairy tale books fell from the shelves and the sprinkler system immediately sprang into action, spraying liquid sugar everywhere to smother any flames.

Red warning lights flashed on Santa's computer, indicating that the explosion had taken place in the chocolate factory. He swallowed hard and a shudder went down his spine.

"Oh goodness, gracious me!" he gasped. Martha, Darfo, Sonya and Johnny were working there today!

Quick as a flash, he grabbed his red coat, pulled on his red hat and dashed off in his big, heavy boots. The elves had downed tools and were heading in the direction of the sirens.

41

The troubled gulps and cries of the butterflies could be heard from afar:

"Ow! Ow! Ow! Ow!"

The little rascals were in danger. Smoke was billowing out of the window into the dark polar night.

"Ow! Ow! Ow! Ow!" cried the butterflies, and their friends hurried to rescue them as fast as they possibly could.

However, no sooner had the first elves reached the big factory doors as Father Christmas could see them smiling and clapping their hands to their heads.

Clap–clap-clap, one after the other!

Puzzled and still worried, Father Christmas reached the scene and took a deep breath.

"Ow! Ow! Ow! Ow!"

Martha, Darfo, Sonya and Johnny were rolling on the floor holding their tummies. The rescuers breathed a big sigh of relief. It was quite common for the chocolate machine to explode when the elves were working there. It happened most every day, which is why Father Christmas had sent the butterflies in – but that had been a total waste of time too! The little rascals were no more able to withstand temptation than were the elves! The magical Chocolate Santa mix was *sooooo* delicious that anyone with a sweet tooth couldn't help but try a spoonful… and a second… and then a third… until the machine finally blew up because the tank was empty!

Ho-hum, it made no difference whether the elves or the butterflies were working in the Chocolate Santa Factory – the magical chocolate mixture had the same effect on all of them!

There they lay on the floor, bellies full and faces green, groaning and feeling sick. Just another normal day at the North Pole!

11

After Work

Complete and utter silence…

The working day was done. Peace and quiet reigned in Santa's Secret City up at the North Pole. Snowmen with wings were dotted all over the place, and the butterflies and elves had built a castle for having snowball fights in.

Father Christmas was sitting in his rocking chair on the veranda after work as usual, slurping on a cup of chocolate tea with a candy floss topping. All was quiet.

All was quiet?

"Hmmm," mumbled Santa, knowing this was probably the lull before the storm!

No sooner had the thought entered his head as the phoenix and the three electric blue fireflies wandered round the corner. Their footsteps left watery trails in front of Father Christmas before freezing back to ice again.

"Jabber, jabber, jabber," the squad chatted away in their vaguely comprehensible dialect, discussing who they thought was the best driver.

A little voice in Santa's head told him to lean forward in his rocking chair to get a better view.

Creaaaaak!

Hey presto, suddenly he could see that the young reindeer were not in their pens.

"Hrrrmph!" he mumbled, lifting his cup. He was about to take another sip when a monstrous noise almost knocked him from his chair:

Whoooooooosh!

Followed by a short silence and then:

"Yipeeeeeee!"

"Dar-fo! Dar-fo! Dar-fo!"

Clack-clack-clack all the brightly coloured floodlights came on, lighting up a stand of snowy seats around Father Christmas, which was full of elves waving their flags.

"Son-ya! Son-ya! Son-ya!" some of them were chanting.

"Joh-nny! Joh-nny! Joh-nny!" shouted others.

The fearless pilots nosedived from the sky, twisting past the chocolate factory, almost knocking down the bakery with their reindeer before racing down the home straight right in front of Santa's house, amid screams from their avid fans.

Everyone agreed that Martha was not likely to be the winner! Her reindeer was dressed in pink and it kept stopping to look at the scenery and sniff the trees, eventually trotting along miles behind Sonya, Johnny and Darfo's reindeer.

They, on the other hand, were going at full pelt, but just before the finish line, they all stopped and waited for their meandering little friend! They didn't go over the line until they were all together.

"Yippeeeee!" the elves cried – no winners, no losers… well, they were all winners.

"Ho, ho, ho!" laughed Santa, blowing on his hot chocolate tea and rocking in his chair.

They all loved a bit of fun up at the North Pole!

12

Magic Stars

A golden comet fell from the sky, shining brighter than the sea of stars. A little more snow fell and covered Santa's Secret City like a layer of icing sugar. Martha and Darfo cuddled up together. They'd finished work for the day and the factory was closed.

"Hee, hee, hee!" giggled the two elves cuddling next to them.

"Have you got room for an old couple?" asked Mrs Claus, as she and Santa joined them. She laid a blanket over everyone's legs.

"Isn't it beautiful out here?" said Mrs Claus, prodding Martha in the side.

"Hee, hee, hee!" Martha giggled, beaming at her. "So you got our invitation?"

"We sure did, we sure did," mumbled Santa, who felt a bit uncomfortable in such a romantic atmosphere.

Mrs Claus, Martha and all the girl elves had declared today the "Girls'-Love-Light-North-Pole-Day' and there were to be no objections! Darfo, powerless to do anything, simply shrugged his shoulders and looked over to Santa.

"That's women for you!" said Santa, leaning back. They had promised him something 'really special', which turned out to be a diversion to stop him thinking of things like 'go and repair the sleigh'!

Soon, all the seats were filled with elf couples, cuddling up to each other to keep warm. Mrs Claus passed pre-heated cups around her group and poured them strawberry tea with a candy floss topping. Then Martha nodded and winked to her, giving the signal to begin. Silence fell among the fairy-tale audience. Then suddenly:

 "Give us a kiss!"

Everyone could hear a voice whisper to Sonja, who promptly gave the offender a kick up the bum... and out tumbled Johnny, landing right in front of everybody! Shocked to be standing in front of an audience, Johnny got up, brushed away the snow and tried to gather himself. He gave a polite bow and cleared his throat.

 "Hear ye, hear ye!" he proclaimed. "Ladies and gentlemen, kissers and snoggers! This evening, I am delighted to be able to present to you the Reindeer Show…" he broke off, pointing at some invisible soul apparently standing behind the wall, and tapped his forehead.

 "Hey, no way am I saying *that*!"

 No-one could tell who the hidden person was, but they could see a butterfly's fists waving about threateningly in the air. Johnny wiped pearls of sweat from his brow.

"Okay, okay!" he said and turned back to the audience, calling:

"And now for Santa's Love-Light Show for Heartbreakers – or those who'd like to become one!" The elves all looked at each other in surprise. Darfo couldn't help but suppress a giggle.

"Hee, hee, hee!"

When Johnny heard the boys laughing, he stomped off behind the wall in a huff... which was the signal for the spectacle in the sky to begin.

It was a dark night. Then, all of a sudden, thousands of stars rained from the sky down to earth, first one or two and then countless stars together. Up above in the sky, the show had begun that everybody would still be talking about years later.

Dasher, Dancer, Prancer, Vixen, Comet, Cupid, Donner and Blitzen appeared out of nowhere, galloping towards the shooting stars, their silver tails streaming behind them. Once they had caught up with the stars, they screeched to a halt. Everyone stared in amazement: they were using their reindeer magic!

The reindeer jumped and danced in front of each shooting star, bringing each one to life with a puff of magic. The golden stars stopped falling and rose back into the sky, only to then fall back to earth again.

This time it was clear to see that on their way back down, they were searching for happy couples. Everyone was staring up at the night sky with their mouths wide open. Each shooting star chose a couple and flew down to them, winding a magic, golden thread around and around them until they were completely bound together.

Making sure they still had enough thread left, the golden stars then leapt up in front of their audience and shot up into the sky, drawing golden heart shapes for all to see, before shooting off forever into the depths of space.

Slowly, the magical, golden threads tightened around the couples, drawing them closer and closer together. They were filled with magical feelings of happiness, trust, comfort, expectation... things that couldn't really be described in words.

How long this condition would last, Johnny and Sonya didn't quite know. Plenty long enough, that was for sure, so they sneaked off to their beds to get some sleep.

Santa and Mrs Claus, Martha and Darfo and all the other elves had no idea how long the feeling would last either. This magical feeling of happiness from the stars was a gift of love that would never die. Christmas was the festival of love, for all eternity...

13

The Secret Christmas Snowball Fight

Whoosh, whoosh, whoosh!
Snowballs were whizzing through the air in Santa's Secret City here at the North Pole.

Zing, zing, zing!
Martha ducked and ran zigzags beneath the oncoming masses of snow, delivering new snow ammunition to her brave team.

They were standing on the north-east tower of Snowball Fight Castle, bombarding their attackers like billy-o. An army of rowdy Christmas elves were threatening to kidnap Princess Sonya if only they could catch her – which would happen any minute now if the brave Knights of the Butterfly failed to protect her. Perish the thought!

 "Grrrr!" growled Martha at the attackers, and SPLAT, a snowball hit her right in the face. Darfo was taken totally unawares by the elves' sneaky attack. He pelted snowball upon snowball at the offending group like a lunatic, but they just kept getting closer and closer – their supply of ammunition seemed endless.

 "We need a change of tactics!" Johnny yelled to Darfo.

 Martha brushed off the snow and ran back down the steps to collect more ammunition. It's a good job she's down there now and not up here, thought Darfo. He couldn't bear to admit to her face that the battle was lost. Then *SMACK, SMACK, SMACK*, he was hit by three snowballs, lost his footing, wobbled and fell over backwards, landing two metres lower in the courtyard, right next to a big pair of black boots.

"Huh?" he gasped, looking up. Martha was grinning down at him, standing next to someone in a red coat with a white beard.

"Ho, ho, ho!" laughed Father Christmas, just as Johnny got hit too, falling down from the battlements into the courtyard. *SPLAT!* He landed in the snow.

"Did anyone order backup troops?" smirked Father Christmas.

Their positive thinking and determination gave them a new boost of energy and the troop stomped back upstairs, opening fire on the Elves. *WHOOSH! SPLAT! SMACK!*

They smothered their opponents in a hail of snowballs. But it was no use: there were just too many of them and Princess Sonya was still in danger. Before they knew it, even Father Christmas had taken four hits to his ample tummy.

'Drat!' grumbled Santa, wishing he'd listened to his wife and had gone on a diet in the summer holidays. So annoyed was he that he turned his wrath on his attackers and *WHOOSH, WHOOSH, WHOOSH,* pelted them with a whole load of snowballs, but it didn't make any difference – the elves just kept getting closer and closer. Princess Sonya would be lost...

SUDDENLY a magic glow appeared in Santa's eyes. Golden rings appeared around his feet that danced up his body, joined together around his tummy and then shot down his arms.
The elves gasped, shocked that Santa was using his magic. Santa clapped his hands together and… the world froze as time stood still.

The elves, Martha, Sonya, Darfo, Johnny, the reindeer, everyone, people watching telly, people taking baths, people sat on buses and even in aeroplanes in the sky – everything stood still, as though turned to stone.

It was the same as the Christmas magic Santa Claus used on Christmas Eve, when he was whizzing about the world in his sleigh. It was the only way he could possibly have time to deliver presents to everyone everywhere. Now he was getting on in years, he'd taken on the butterflies to help him, as even his magic didn't quite give him enough time to do everything all by himself.

"Now let's see who's winning!" he called, leaping over the castle wall and covering every elf from head to toe in snow. Then he ran back to the castle, up the stairs and stood next to the butterflies before clapping his hands together again and restarting time.

"Boo! Hiss! Boo!" the elves called from below. Darfo, Martha and Sonya looked at each other, stunned. None of the elves were throwing snowballs anymore! They freed themselves from the masses of snow and skulked away, beaten.

"Yipeeeee!" celebrated the butterflies. They had won. They stuck their chests out and proudly marched back and forth in front of the losers.

Mrs Claus wasn't overly impressed by the outcome of the battle.

"What's wrong?" asked Santa. "You know I needed to practise for the big day!"

14

Ice Skating à la Butterfly

WHIZZ! WHIZZ! WHIZZ!

The elves, Butterflies, Santa and Mrs Claus shot around the frozen secret lake in Santa's Secret City at the North Pole. Snowflakes were dancing through the air, being wafted around by the ice skaters. Countless torch flames created a romantic atmosphere at the lake's edge. The Christmas Elves' Philharmonic played Christmas carols on their violins.

The electric blue fireflies and the phoenix were so drawn in by the music that they fluttered away from the bank of the lake above the ice, floating around between the skaters.

It was such a picture of joy and happiness, not a care in the world... until the phoenix forgot to keep flying and, to everyone's horror, landed on the ice, spinning around wildly like the star of some ice skating show.

"Help!!!" the phoenix called out in utter panic.

"Hey! Hey!" Martha called.

The others looked up to see Martha pointing energetically at the madly spinning phoenix, who was causing clouds of steam to come off the melting lake every time he put a fiery foot down. *Fizzzzzzzzzz...*

Too late!

CRACKKKK, CRACKKKK! The ice began to break up.

"Oh my goodness!"

The firebird leapt into the sky as soon as he noticed the ice was cracking into floes, some small, some large. Santa and Mrs Claus were right in the middle of the lake!

The Butterflies could use their wings to carry themselves out of the danger zone, but the elves and Santa and Mrs Claus didn't have that option and were in severe peril of falling into the freezing cold water. Oh no, who'd have thought this might happen? Christmas was in danger!!!

A visitor ambled to the lakeside, plumped her ample bottom down in the snow and pulled on her ice skates at a leisurely pace. The elves, butterflies and the phoenix waved frantically to her to go and get a rope, just as Mrs Claus was slithering to the other end of her ice floe. Father Christmas had caused it to sink at his end due to his weight and now Mrs Claus was sliding uncontrollably towards him, only just managing to catch hold of his legs at the last minute. Fortunately Father Christmas's boots had the best grip on them that any butterfly had ever seen and he didn't budge an inch.

The woman at the lakeside made no attempt to go and get a rope, or even a branch.

Is she completely bonkers, thought Johnny the Macho Butterfly, looking at Darfo. He shrugged his shoulders. The woman was too far away for them to be able to see who she was.

Martha leapt up and began to fly across to her as quickly as possible… and then stopped in mid-flight to wave to her.

"Has she gone totally bonkers too?" asked Sonya, scratching her head as she saw the panic in Mrs Claus's eyes. She wouldn't be able to hold on for much longer.

The elves were in a sorry state and one of them had actually fallen into the water. Their floes were swaying and wobbling to and fro… when the woman, who had at last managed to get her ice skates on, finally went down to the edge of the lake and noticed that the ice was broken.

"Tut, tut – that's just no good at all," she mumbled and put her index finger in her mouth. Then she held her finger up into the air. If you'd been standing close to her, you'd have seen that her finger lit up crystal blue.

"That's right," she said to her hand. She bent over and put her magic index finger into the water. *CRUNCH, CREAK, CRUNCH!*

A new, thick coat of ice spread out before her.

"Phewwww!" everybody gasped, relieved. In no time at all, the whole lake was frozen back over again. Now they knew who she was!

"Ooops!" said Santa, as his disgruntled wife slid off their floe onto the newly formed ice.

"I'd completely forgotten that Mother Hulda was coming to visit us today!"

15

White Christmas

Whole loads of snow fell up here on Santa's Secret City at the North Pole. The snowflakes floated gently on the breeze, landing wherever the wind took them. One of them chose to land right on Martha's nose, who giggled and tried to lick it off. *Lick! Slurp!*

"Oh come on, slow coach!" Darfo waved up and down impatiently and the butterfly girl hopped into the sleigh. Santa's sleigh. With a mixed team pulling it.

Dasher, Dancer, Prancer, Vixen, Comet, Cupid, Donner and Blitzen were with the front sleigh; behind them were the other butterflies' sleighs and reindeer, all joined together with ropes.

The sleighs were so heavily laden that the little rascals were not able to steer the front one all by themselves, so they sat with Father Christmas.

They had a good reason for this set-up. The first three sleighs were full of presents and the last two were full of carrots and candy floss, which were used to cajole the teams into action.

"Be sure to be back in time for tea," said Mrs Claus, pinching Santa's cheek as he looked at her lovingly.

"We will be, we will be!" he promised his wife.

The Christmas elves waved once more before taking off with their sleighs and setting to work. Santa and the butterflies were going away on business – it was certainly no holiday!

Once they'd gone through the check list, Ol' Whitebeard took the reins and pressed the red 'hover' button. The Christmas convoy shot up into the sky to a big "*HO, HO, HO!*"

"I'm sure we'll get it all done," Johnny whispered to Sonya, who nodded positively.

Father Christmas drove Dasher, Dancer, Prancer, Vixen, Comet, Cupid, Donner and Blitzen higher and ever higher, working them really hard. They didn't mind one bit because they knew they were granting children's wishes: it was for the well-being of mankind.

"I've wished for some heart-shaped ones," Martha whispered to Darfo, who squeezed her hand happily. It was quite romantic sitting there in the red and green sleigh… well, at least until the three electric blue fireflies appeared from between the piles of presents behind them and joined them on the front bench.

Johnny and Sonja looked at the stowaways in surprise, when *PLOP,* the phoenix appeared next to them out of nowhere with a cheeky grin. It was understandable that they all wanted to be part of this mission!

It was a bit of a squeeze to fit in, but nobody minded. Before long they were flying through a thick blanket of clouds, rattling their way right to the centre of High Cloud City.

As soon as Dasher, Dancer, Prancer, Vixen, Comet, Cupid, Donner and Blitzen noticed that they had reached their destination, they slowed down and Santa pressed the red and green hover button.

They landed on the clouds and slid gently before coming to a standstill.

Nestling atop the cloud was a gold-glowing palace. The palace gates were open: their visit was expected.

Santa parked the convoy of sleighs so that they could still be seen from inside.

HOP, HOP, HOP! They all hopped out of their sleighs and, awestruck, entered the massive audience room. Their host had already taken his place behind his desk. Next to him sat his colleague Mother Hulda, an elderly lady with white hair and a rather large bottom.

Darfo was about to take the lead in front of Santa – he'd been here loads of times before and knew his way around. Martha held him back with a smile. *Today,* that was Santa's job!

The Christmas Chief greeted the Chief Weather Maker, St. Peter, with a big "Ho! Ho! Ho!" and nodded to Mother Hulda, who was sitting next to him. Mother Hulda gave her friend Martha a secret little wave and Martha nodded back.

"Sit down, sit down!" said St. Peter, lifting his arms and *PING, PING, PING,* enough chairs for everybody appeared out of nowhere.

"How's your wife?" St. Peter asked Santa with a smile.

"Fine thanks, and she's still cooking as well as she did when I first met her," he replied.

"I can see that!" said St. Peter, looking at Santa's tummy, laughing. Mother Hulda gave him a glare. Darfo and Johnny looked at one another – surely there was something going on between those two, *"Tee, hee, hee!"*

"Right, let's get down to business, this time it's not just a social call!"

"I can see that," said St. Peter, pointing to the sleighs outside the palace gates. "What can I do for you?"

"Well this year is quite unusual... there's one particular gift that is at the top of every child's wish list!"

"Well I don't make toys, you know…" said St. Peter, shrugging his shoulders and licking his lips at the sight of the candy floss. Ooh great butterflies, he could just eat some of that! Martha and Darfo grinned at one other. There was a very good reason for supplying him with super-duper ultra-high-quality candy floss all year round... and for stopping those deliveries just a few days ago!

"Well no, I wasn't talking about toys, I was talking about..."

"Come on, spit it out!" the Chief Weather Maker urged impatiently, glancing back and forth between the candy floss and his visitors.

"Oh well, okay... we're here to collect a guaranteed white Christmas off you!"

St. Peter looked up in shock and fidgeted about in his chair... until Mother Hulda lovingly squeezed his hand under the table.

"Oooh!" thought the butterflies, being small enough to be able to see under the table. They opened their eyes wide: *"Caught them!!!"*

"But...but...but...but... you know I can't promise that!" stammered St. Peter.

Santa, however, signalled to him with his eyes that there are ways and means of doing everything.

Martha and Darfo were much less tactful and pointed straight at the red telephone on his desk.

"You only need to make one call!"

He glanced first at the candy floss, then at his visitors and then at Mother Hulda. She nodded gently. *The children, it's for the children*, the most beautiful face of all the heavens said to him.

"Hmmmm," he hesitated for a second and then reached for the handset. A phone automatically

65

rang a few storeys higher and somebody answered it.

"Uh, this is, uh, St. Peter... oh, you already know? Oh yes, of course… uh, boss, Father Christmas and the butterflies are here with me... oh, you know that too? Yes, erm, they want to know… oh, you already know that too, really? …I should do that? Aha, oho, hmmm, …not for ages, hmm, yes, okay, alright boss, mmm, okay? …Not a word... okay, I've got that, thank you!"

St. Peter hung up and turned back round. Stunned, the butterflies gawped at the Chief Weather Maker. The electric blue fireflies flicked their ears to snap them out of the trance.

"Oooh!" they came to their senses just in time to see St. Peter signing a letter, which Mother Hulda adorned with the High Cloud City seal. *SPLAT!* Then she passed the envelope back to St. Peter, who was by now a bit more relaxed and finding great comfort in eyeing up the candy floss sleigh:

"That load stays *right here*!"

"Of course, of course" stammered the Butterflies. The Chief Weather Maker turned back to Father Christmas. "This," he said, pointing at the envelope, "is for every child on earth, to be delivered by you."

Santa nodded calmly – that was all part of his job. Then he got up, bowed and turned to leave High Cloud City.

"Hang on a minute!" said Darfo. "What about our white Christmas???"

St. Peter understood the little butterfly's impatience and grinned, pointing to the envelope in Santa's hand.

"It's all in there, be it this year or next, it's all in there!"

Darfo jumped up and ran to Father Christmas. With great leaping bounds into the air, he caught a glimpse of the secret letter. He could just make out some writing at the top of it. Father Christmas grabbed the envelope and quickly stuffed it inside his coat. He shrugged his shoulders and made for his sleigh.

"Sorry, my friend, we won't be opening THAT until 24th December, the Festival of Love."

16

Intruders at Christmas Tree Forest

INTRUDER ALERT! INTRUDER ALERT!
The sirens sounded out across Santa's Secret City at the North Pole. Flashing red lights lit up corridors, offices, factories and bedrooms and a high-pitched alarm howled out a blood curdling tone.

Dragged from their sleep, Martha, Darfo, Sonya and Johnny rubbed their eyes and looked around in confusion. They jumped out of bed and ran up the spiral staircase in the middle of the room before leaping onto the fireman's pole. They spun down to the ground to await further orders.

The door sprang open and an elf ran in:

"It's not a practice drill! The alarm's gone off at Christmas Tree Forest!!!"

"No way!" The little rascals were fuming. They set off straight away, pulling on their winter clothes as they ran.

Santa was just about to set off in his sleigh as they reached him.

"Quick! All aboard!" he boomed in his deep voice. The butterflies scrambled up as the reindeer accelerated. Higher and higher they went up into the sky, though they still managed to clip the tiles on the chocolate factory roof, causing a minor snow slide.

It wasn't far to Christmas Tree Forest.

"If it's caught fire, we'll soon put it out!" speculated Darfo, at the same time wondering what kind of shady character might have set fire to the most beautiful trees of the year.

"Maybe it was the trolls?"

"Who knows!" he replied.

A wild conversation started as to how and why anyone would want to do such a thing.

"*Babble, babble, babble!*"

No sooner had they reached the first trees as they could hear the sound of chainsaws.

"Tree thieves!" hissed Sonya the Butterfly Warrior, clenching her fists.

Father Christmas guided Dasher, Dancer, Prancer, Vixen, Comet, Cupid, Donner and Blitzen in the direction of the noise. Several evil-looking figures wearing dark balaclavas were creeping around with torches. The flames from their torches lit up their misdeeds.

CRASHHHHH!

The rescue squad witnessed another tree falling to the ground. A surge of anger ran through their bodies from top to toe. Everyone in the sleigh was furious.

The sleigh shot towards the gangsters with a loud "*HO, HO, HO!*"

Everyone in the sleigh could see Father Christmas pressing the only-to-be-used-in-an-utter-emergency button...

The sleigh turned into a wild, living, fire spewing, silver dragon that headed straight for the criminals!

When the first shady character saw what was coming his way, he could hardly believe his eyes and shouted to warn his mates. They pointed up at the monstrous dragon, freezing with fright for a moment before flinging away their chainsaws and torches and running for their lives, through the snow, in the darkness, towards their getaway trucks. They were absolutely petrified.

"We'll never come back here again," Santa and the butterflies heard them say as they slammed their truck doors and raced off out of the woods towards the main road.

"Fire at them!" Johnny squawked, glaring at Santa.

"Ho, ho, ho!" Santa nodded grimly and steered the Christmas dragon towards the last truck.

Whooooosh! The silvery monster breathed a wall of fire at the vehicle, which stopped just short of the driver's cabin. The terrified screams of the criminal echoed out into the night, alerting the trucks in front, who could see what was happening in their wing mirrors.

"That'll do!" said Martha the butterfly girl happily, placing her hand on Santa's arm. "I think they've had quite enough!"

He gave her a gentle smile and, turning the dragon back into a sleigh, flew back to the scene of the crime. They landed in a clearing and got out. They could all feel the pain and sorrow coming from the Christmas trees, for this was of course a *magical* Christmas tree forest.

"Four trees!" said Darfo, listing the number of casualties. Santa nodded. He turned to his friends with a bitter face and a trembling voice.

"An unforgiveable crime has occurred!" he called loudly into the forest, turning to look at every tree as he spoke. The trees stood tall and proud with their solid, brown trunks and cloaks of green needles.

"We will bury the victims." he called, a little quieter.

The butterflies could hear creaking and cracking sounds coming from the forest. Martha clambered up closer to Darfo. Had she just seen a branch move? And there! And another one?

"We're so very sorry!" said Santa.

And there! Another movement amongst the trees! And there! And another and another... and one more! The snow was piling up beneath the trees. It looked like the roots were lifting up.

CRACK, CRUNCH!

The snow was brushed aside as the great, thick tree roots rose out of the ground – the Christmas trees were lifting themselves up, snow falling from their branches at every move.

Martha, Darfo, Johnny and Sonya stood there, mouths wide open.

"If you lift your roots and run away, they'll still find you!"

Santa spoke to the trees as though it was the most natural thing in the world. The butterflies began to get over the fact that the magical Christmas trees were alive. Nothing was impossible, that they knew for sure.

Martha the butterfly girl was the first to get used to the idea. Delighted at the very thought, she fluttered over to Santa and excitedly whispered something in his ear. He nodded, impressed.

"Good idea!" he mumbled positively. Cracking sounds were still coming from the woods.

"They will continue to chop trees down at this festive time!" Ol' Whitebeard declared to his forest, his red coat and hat visible from afar. "And so it is my wish and the wish of all the butterflies, the elves and Mrs Claus that you come with us. Come with us to our Secret City. There you will be safe!"

The cracking noises stopped abruptly as the Christmas trees stopped moving. Mutterings and rustlings whispered through the branches. They were consulting one another... and then the biggest, fullest, most beautiful tree at the front turned to face them. It glistened in the night sky. Then its needles lit up with a blueish glow and let off small, glittering stars which flew up into the air, at first dancing around alone before gathering into groups. Then all the other trees released their magic stars too. The stars joined together in front of Father Christmas and the butterflies and then whizzed up into the sky to draw a picture for them – a picture of Santa's Secret City, the elves, Santa, the butterflies, the reindeer and everything else - plus something new: there were magical Christmas trees everywhere, between the houses, by Snowball Fight Castle, by the chocolate factory – simply everywhere! So their answer was – *YES!!!*

"Hooray" the butterflies cried, hugging each other and throwing their arms around Father Christmas. *Cuddle time!!!* Santa was a bit embarrassed and interrupted them:

"Right, my friends! Let's go!" he called, heading for the sleigh.

The magic Christmas trees ended their show and followed the Christmas troop.

"But what about the baddies? Won't they notice there's something strange going on here?" Darfo asked Father Christmas as they sat on the front bench of the sleigh flying home.

"Don't worry," Santa grinned. "Do you really think anybody would believe them?"

17

The Spooky Christmas Spirit

The stars shone gently in the night sky above the North Pole. Snow fell softly and covered the sleeping Christmas trees. The elves put their lights out. Santa could be heard snoring a duet with Mrs Claus.

"SNORE-*snore*, SNORE-*snore*, SNORE-*snore*!"

All was calm in Santa's Secret City.

Darfo clambered up the ladder to the top bunk, Sonya cuddled up under the blankets in her bunk and Johnny sneaked a little firecracker under

Martha's pillow whilst she was standing looking out of the window at the peaceful scenery.

"Ahhh!" she sighed in a dreamy voice before tiptoeing back to bed.

They'd worked really hard today. They'd made and wrapped endless presents, then they'd trained the reindeer for the big day and fed them carrots for tea. A truly successful day.

A thought crossed Darfo's mind just as the butterfly girl was about to go back to bed.

"Did you set up the magic Christmas chocolate dehypomeasurator? I always find it a real nuisance when it's floating at the ceiling the next morning and then we have to fill it all up again. After that, I'm always so full that I don't feel like working."

"What's put that in your mind?" Martha wanted to know as she put her foot on the first rung of the ladder.

"Can't you hear it rattling?"

The butterflies all held their breath and listened. He was right, they thought. So it was!

"But," said Johnny squinting suspiciously, "that's not the machine!"

"Not the machine?" Martha hopped back to the floor and ran to the window.

Three, two, one… Darfo, Johnny and Sonya raced up next to her and inspected their view over the Secret City.

Clatter, rattle, rattle! It sounded like someone kicking a bucket over in the dark.

Sonya jumped.

"The thieves are here!"

She shuddered with fear at the thought. *Help!!!*

Darfo and Martha were just running up the spiral staircase as Johnny showed Sonya something outside the window.

"Look! Something white! Something white is creeping through the night!"

Martha and Darfo ran back down quickly and pressed their noses against the window pane.

"Where? Where?"

"There!" pointed Darfo. And so it was. Now they could all see it.

"It… it… it… might be a Christmas Spirit trying to cast spells on the presents!"

Sonya and Johnny looked on in shock, rolling up their pyjama sleeves and shaking their fists.

"We'll show *him!*"

They grabbed their boots and pulled them on in a whizz. Martha and Darfo were a bit unsure but followed suit and then everyone put on their winter coats.

"Should… should we tell Father Christmas? I mean, just to be on the safe side?"

"Piffle! I know all about ghosts!" Johnny boasted.

"You're right!" Sonya giggled, without touching on the details of his last encounter.

"Pfff!" he muttered, as the group bravely marched outside. No sooner had their boots crunched into the snow as the strange noise stopped. The lights from Snowball Fight Castle lit up the lane before them. They all stood still and listened carefully. Within four seconds, another clatter – the ghost was still there!

Crunch, crunch, crunch, the group started to walk again and the noises stopped abruptly. They stood still for a moment.

Boing! Boing! Boing!

"What, a ghost that's using our trampoline to bounce about all over the place?"

"He's bounced around that long, he's going to break it!" Johnny declared, running off. The only place the Christmas Spirit could be at was the elves' playhouse. That was the only place where toys were stored that were actually allowed to be played with.

When they arrived at the door, the butterflies lined up with their backs to the wall like members of some kind of super-duper-ultra-cool secret service unit. Darfo waved his hands about, giving instructions in sign language.

"What? You want to teach a Christmas tree to tango?" Johnny looked at him in confusion.

"Sshhh!"

He shook his head and signed again.

"Huh? You want to take a bath with a raccoon whilst burping the alphabet?"

"Ohhhhh!" He groaned and said out loud, "We're going in – three, two, one!"

He turned around and kicked the door.

"Ouch!"

He fell backwards into the snow. The door was still shut tight. Martha walked over and pressed down the handle.

"On the other hand, you could just do this!" she giggled.

Darfo got up and shook himself. Luckily, they knew the ghost wouldn't be able to get out – this was the only door.

The noises started again.

Splat, splat, rattle, rattle, rattle!

Martha was disgusted. Someone was using their water colour paints!

Forgetting to be scared, she ran to the light switches, fuming.

Click – click – click! The room lit up. The butterflies stared in astonishment.

Two geese and their three goslings were gathered around dozens of sheets of paper, scribbling and scrawling away at something. The sudden light made them jump. Mrs Goose and the goslings hurriedly hid behind Mr Goose. Two of the goslings began to cry.

"Oh dearie me!" Sonya exclaimed.

Martha stopped being cross and was close to tears.

Darfo took a look around and walked towards them with his hands held high.

"We... we... we come in peace!"

But the geese continued to takes steps backwards until the goslings' backs were against the wall. They began to panic – they were captured again, despite Mr Goose having said that they would never again have to go back in a cage!

He summoned up all his courage, prepared to fight to the death if it meant saving his children. Sonya and Martha stood looking at the pieces of paper in amazement.

"Come here! Come here! Come and look at this!"

The geese relaxed a little as Darfo and Johnny hurried back over to the girls. They too were amazed - they could see quite clearly what the geese had been painting!

The geese had painted pictures of themselves escaping from cages. Next to them was a painting of a Christmas tree and a family sat at the dinner table with knives and forks. The father of the family was missing in that picture – he was in another picture chasing geese with an axe! Another sheet of paper showed the goose family out alone at night in the freezing cold, looking for a new home. They had just finished painting that picture when they were interrupted by the butterflies.

"They're… they're seeking asylum!" Sonya gasped.

The butterflies looked at the goose family in amazement. The geese edged a little closer. Mrs Goose looked at Martha hopefully. Her warm, brown eyes could have melted an iceberg… and they certainly melted the butterfly girl's heart like butter. With arms open wide, she ran to Mrs Goose and gave her a big hug.

"Of course you can stay!" Martha sniffed.

Father Christmas interrupted her with a "Ho, ho, ho!"

He had appeared suddenly in the doorway, accompanied by the Elf Guards.

"I think *I* have a say in this matter!"

Everyone froze in shock. Suddenly a hand reached out from the crowd and slapped Santa on the back of his head – ouch!

"You can stop your silly games!" Mrs Claus snapped as she squeezed through to the front. "Of course they can stay – forever if they like… under one condition!" she said as she strode up to them. Everyone stared at Mrs Claus questioningly.

"You will have to help us to prepare for Christmas!"

Not a problem was written all over Mrs Goose's face.

The goslings had already started playing chase with the phoenix and the three electric blue fireflies.

Mr Goose was beaming: a promise was a promise, and let's face it, these were not humans. He put the tips of his feathers to his beak and called out loudly: "Honk, honk!"

This was the signal! Everyone turned around and looked in amazement at the commotion between the Christmas trees. There were families of geese everywhere, gaggling as they ran into the Secret City at the North Pole. First they hugged Santa, then Mrs Claus, then the elves and then the butterflies. They were sobbing with joy – they had all been rescued!

The goose family joined in last. Joy was all around – without even having to use magic!

You see, Christmas wouldn't be Christmas if it wasn't the Festival of Love, now, would it?

18

Someone's Always There

The snow fell softly in the darkness, covering the Secret City at the North Pole. The Christmas trees swayed in their sleep and the elves' green suits were hanging up outside to air. Happy snoring sounds came from the all-new Christmas Goose House.

Santa was sitting in his rocking chair on the veranda, drinking strawberry and chocolate tea with jelly bears, feeling rather pleased with himself. It would soon be Christmas and everything was running to plan. He knew only too well that the geese had helped a great deal towards getting things done on time. Had it only been himself and the elves as in years gone by, well, they probably wouldn't have got finished in time this year. Santas get older too, you know.

"Aaah!" he sighed contentedly, taking his cup in both hands and blowing away the steam.

The butterflies. Things may get a bit chaotic when they were around, but they did actually get twice as much work done by the end of the day. The little rascals were a blessing in disguise!

He slowly sipped on his tea, watching the reindeer. He couldn't stop wondering: *had they really thought of everything?*

Santa let go of his cup with one hand to scratch his white hair under his red hat. He couldn't get over the feeling that he'd forgotten something. Everyone knows that feeling.

There was something else left to do, definitely something else… but what was it?

Mrs Claus walked up behind him and put her arm around him. "Every year you get all worried and every year everything turns out to be fine!" she said. They gazed out across the horizon together.

"You may well be right, my dear!"

He squeezed her hand. It was nice and warm. He was just about to peck her on the cheek when he thought of something.

"But then again, perhaps you're wrong!"

Had they forgotten to switch the machines on? Mrs Claus and Santa both peered out suspiciously into the night. There was definitely something…

They looked around frantically. The reindeer were in their pens and the geese were so tired that they certainly wouldn't still be on the go. And as for the elves… well, after their chocolate and candy floss feast earlier, they had only just managed to clamber into their beds!

"What about Martha, Darfo, Sonya and Johnny?" Santa and Mrs Claus looked at one another. *The butterflies!*

Father Christmas leapt out of his rocking chair and leaned over the veranda railings to look around the corner. All was quiet at Butterfly House. Not a sound!

Not a sound! Their eyes widened. That was very suspicious indeed – at least one of the butterflies was always normally wandering around. They never all seemed to sleep at the same time. You could hear them crunching through the snow, or having pillow fights, or Martha was fluttering around on a secret date.

Santa and Mrs Claus pulled on their heavy outdoor coats and had just arrived at Butterfly House when there was a muffled crack and a glittery blue flash coming from the toy factory behind it.

Huh?

They walked around the house quickly. There was no point stopping to see whether any butterflies were in it!

Whizz, bang, puff! There it was again.

"Whatever can that be?" Mrs Claus whispered as they looked across at the toy factory. They stood still, eyes wide open.

The middle of the roof was open – there was a big gap in it and flashes of lightning were shooting about all over the place. There were bright rings of light, in every colour of the rainbow. And there were Martha and Darfo, wearing white laboratory coats, standing on the roof looking angrily into the sky, waving their hands about wildly.

Santa and Mrs Claus still couldn't work out what was happening and crept up a bit closer. They could see Johnny and Sonya's silhouettes through the window, and they were close enough now to hear what was going on.

"But you promised us!" Martha complained, pointed her finger at the sky and waving. "We've only got time to do it today – they have to soak for a few days. And it has to be fresh dust, not the dust you already gave us!"

Suddenly the heavens began to move, as though they had understood every word. The stars left their places in the sky and started to move around. First one, then another, and another, and then one more.

The stars followed the calls of the little butterfly girl and started to fall down to earth. They sank lower and lower until they almost crashed into the ground at the North Pole.

Santa and Mrs Claus were standing by the wall at his point and could see Johnny and Sonya scuttling around a big pan, which they'd apparently brought with them from the Christmas bakery. Johnny poured in one mystery ingredient after another whilst Sonya stirred the mixture with a big wooden spoon. Blue clouds of dust billowed into the air, accompanied by flashes of light in all directions.

Luckily Santa and Mrs Claus were stood in a place where they could see up through the gap and across the roof. Martha and Darfo stood at the edge as the shooting stars headed straight for the factory.

The first two stars purred softly into the factory and did a lap of honour, giggling. Then they seemed to be chasing each other, but suddenly they sprinted apart before dashing towards one another at top speed. They crashed into each other directly above the big pan, causing fresh, golden star dust to cascade into it. No sooner had those two stars returned to the night sky in a steep flight as the next two stars entered the factory. This procedure went on and on and Father Christmas could hardly believe his eyes.

"So you did forget something!" Mrs Claus exclaimed, prodding her husband in the side and dragging him away from the factory.

"What, I *did* forgot something?"

"Yes – the people who feel lonely at Christmas. I remember my grandmother telling me," she whispered in his ear, "that only the butterflies can help them. They're born with the gift of being able to change how people feel."

"How?" asked Santa, puzzled.

"It's a unique method – they bake feelings and give them as Christmas gifts! They give the lonely people the certainty that there is always somebody there for them in the world, even if they've lost them or they haven't found them yet. Someone's always there."

Her husband put his arms around her, pressing his scratchy beard to her cheek and gave her a kiss.

"Someone's always there!" he said.

19

Mrs Claus's Secret

All was quiet by the frozen lake. The trees glistened festively in the Secret City at the North Pole. It was nearly Christmas.

Sniff, sniff, sniff!

A delighted Father Christmas opened his eyes and wiggled his toes under the bedclothes. A sweet smell was wafting up his nose.

"Ho, ho, ho!"

He knew that smell! Mrs Claus was in the kitchen baking good morning muffins for breakfast. They somehow smelled a bit different today, but delicious nonetheless.

He sat up and his magic slippers leapt onto his feet... *Huh?* Just a moment... Santa looked down.

"*Snore, snore!*"

"*Zzz, Zzz!*"

Second attempt... SANTA'S SLIPPERS LEAPT ONTO HIS FEET!

"Oh goodness gracious!" said the slippers, prizing their eyes open and dashed towards Santa, leaping onto his waiting feet.

Now another working day could begin. He put on his dressing gown, which was covered in pictures of baubles, and scuffled into the kitchen.

Mrs Claus was just putting the tenth layer of icing onto the muffins. He gave her a kiss on the back of the neck and went into the bathroom.

First he brushed his teeth with chocolate toothpaste and then he took his red trousers and red shirt off the radiator and got dressed. Finally he pulled on his socks and boots – ready!

"Aaah!" Santa stretched and was just thinking how nice it was that everything was so calm and quiet this late in the morning.

So quiet this late in the morning???

He dashed to the front door and stuck his head out. Nothing to be heard? At this time of the morning? It was normally all systems go by now!

The butterflies weren't always that punctual, but the elves worked from dawn till dusk. And the sun had definitely been up in the sky for quite some time, of that he was sure.

What was going on?

From where he was standing, he could see the reindeer shaking like leaves and he could hear them clearing their throats.

"Uh-oh!" he boomed, expecting the worst.

He ran to the elves' living quarters and heard exactly the same noises.

"Cough! Sneeze! Choke!"

Oh my goodness, he thought. He ripped the door open… all the elves were lying in their beds moaning and groaning. They were far too poorly to be able to get up. Oh no! It was the North Pole Flu - what a disaster!!!

He turned on his heels and ran to the butterflies. No sooner had he reached the door as he could hear them too.

"Achoo! *Zing!* Achoo! *Zing!* Achoo! *Zing!*"

He peered round the door. Johnny, Darfo and Sonya were bobbed down facing backwards, wearing roller skates. They all had bright red noses and were wrapped up warm. Martha was serving them cup upon cup of hot honey.

"Achoo!" Darfo sneezed, shooting past Johnny on his skates, "*Zing!*"

"Achoo!" sneezed Johnny, catching him up, "*Zing!*"

They had marked out a finish line at the end of the room, in the hope that whoever crossed it first would get better first. This was obviously some kind of magical butterfly procedure known only to the butterflies and the universe!

Santa heard yet another "Achoo!" and turned around in dismay, almost knocking Mrs Claus over. She stood there with a tray of muffins and smiled at him, but she could see the panic in his eyes.

"What on earth are we going to go? Christmas is in danger!"

"Well," she said, pushing him aside gently. "Let mummy deal with things and just be patient!"

He moved out of her way and looked worriedly at Darfo, Martha, Johnny and Sonya. Mrs Claus gave them each one of her muffins. They lifted up their hands limply to take them but they didn't feel a bit hungry.

"Come along, eat up and things will soon look a lot better!"

It was more of an order than a request. They looked up suspiciously at Mrs Claus and then down at the muffins.

"Achoo!"

Darfo was first to shoot across the magical finish line and decided to eat his muffin.

No sooner had he swallowed the first bite as he began to feel warmer and warmer and warmer.

94

"Hot! Hot! Hot!"

He leapt out of his roller skate and ran towards the bathroom. The more he ran, the more went down into his stomach and filled him with super-hero energy. All the aches and pains had gone and he felt strong and healthy. His head, nose and lungs were all clear.

He took a deep breath and fluttered up into the air, did a somersault and shot past his friends to the toy factory, ready to get back to work. Martha, Johnny and Sonya had watched all this happen and HEY PRESTO, the muffins soon disappeared into their tummies too! It wasn't long before they also shot back to work like little rockets.

Santa looked at his wife in sheer disbelief.

"How… what… how…" he stammered.

"See!" Mrs Claus grinned at her husband and walked away, wiggling her behind. "I have my secrets too, you know!"

20

Sabotage at Santa's City

 A lot of snow fell here at the North Pole, on Santa's Secret City. The friendly Christmas trees swayed in the breeze and the phoenix used his fiery glow to melt ice, which he used to make more sculptures in the snow. The electric blue fireflies were playing catch and troops of worker geese could be seen marching about all over the place. Everything seemed deceptively peaceful.

 It was only a few days until Christmas and each day, something new seemed to break. First, the oven in the Christmas bakery broke down, then some of the conveyor belts in the toy factory stopped working. Then the red hover buttons on Santa's sleigh and all the butterflies' sleighs were sticking - whereas the glue on the wrapping paper wasn't!

 All these events were happing far too often and it didn't take a genius to work out that it must be SABOTAGE! To start with they were just plain angry, but once they'd calmed down, they created a Special Investigations Committee made up of Martha, Darfo, Johnny, Sonya and Father Christmas.

And so it came that Martha, Sonya, Johnny and Santa were sitting on one side of the table in the dark interrogation room and Darfo on the other. The blinding interrogation lamp was pointing right in his face.

"Admit it! You want to sabotage Christmas because you want to keep all the presents to yourself!"

"Bahhhh!" Darfo crossed his arms in front of his chest. "You're all mad!"

"Well give us one reason why we should believe you!" snapped Martha the butterfly girl.

"I would have thought that was obvious! Because I love the children we'll be delivering the presents to!"

Whisper, whisper, whisper! The interrogation team confided in one another – and waved him through.

"Okay! You're innocent!"

Darfo was delighted and dashed to change places with Martha. She had to squint in the bright light the moment she sat down in front of the interrogators. Great butterfly, it was really hot in here! The interrogation started straight away.

"Admit it, you nasty Christmas saboteur! You want to destroy the Festival of Love because you don't feel loved enough yourself!" Johnny the Macho Butterfly pointed at her and Father Christmas nodded.

"Pffff!" Martha glared at them, tapping her head. Then she pulled the polo neck of her jumper down to reveal lots of chocolatey kiss marks. Darfo went bright red.

"I think that's sufficient proof!" she jibed.

Mutter, mutter, mutter! The team confided again – and waved her through.

Johnny and Sonja had to go through the same procedure too, whereupon the interrogation experts agreed that the former was not bright enough to plan such elaborate acts of sabotage, and the latter was far too preoccupied with herself to be spending any amount of time making such plans.

Then it was Santa's turn.

"Do I really have to?"

"Well it can't have been the elves, the geese, the phoenix or the fireflies, because it just wasn't them." the butterflies said, pointing to the chair. Santa sat down in the bright light. It was so bright that it lit up nearly all of him and he began to sweat immediately. He fiddled nervously with the pom-pom on his hat with one hand and rubbed his leg with the other. He kept looking up to the left and then up to the right. The butterflies were well-known for their secret interrogation methods. They had quite a reputation. They could get everything out of you.

Help! Santa thought. If he didn't admit to it, he would end up looking really silly, and there was no way he wanted that to happen. Whatever would Mrs Claus say? He would have to admit it: he had no other choice.

Darfo and Johnny wanted to play the bad cops and Martha and Sonya the good ones. Santa had just put his hands in the air and had begun to open his mouth when suddenly the Total Emergency Siren went off!

"*Eeee-oooh, Eeee-oooh, Eeee-oooh!*"

The siren screamed out and red warning lights were flashing everywhere.

"Huh?"

They all turned around as the door opened and the captain of the elf guards came in.

"You can stop all that! We have the culprit!" he grinned, running back out again.

The butterflies and Santa hurtled out after him.

"Phew!" Father Christmas heaved a sigh of relief: no-one had noticed the amount of chocolate missing due to his secret midnight feasts! He simply couldn't resist it, but at least his little secret was safe. He opened the front the door. Outside in the daylight, the reindeer and geese were in a circle around one of the Christmas trees. As Santa's group came closer, they could see a cage too.

"Our trap, the one hidden under the Christmas tree!"

Johnny rejoiced and Sonya clapped his hand in a high-five. That had been their idea, though of course Father Christmas was in on the secret.

They had set up secret candy floss traps, because NOBODY could resist the candy floss unless they'd already had three large portions that day. As everyone who lived in Santa's Secret City could eat as much candy floss as they liked, according to butterfly logic, it followed that anybody who couldn't resist the temptation and ended up in the trap MUST be an outsider and therefore the saboteur.

Yet when the little rascals finally managed to push their way to the front to get a better look, they and Father Christmas were totally surprised! The irritated elves were already clapping their hands to their heads because in the cage was... the Easter Bunny, wearing a white camouflage suit and carrying a spare pack of carrots, sat there mumbling away to himself – again.

"Ho, ho, ho!" boomed Santa, unable to think of anything else to say.

Every year just before Christmas, the Easter Bunny sneaked in and smashed things up, just because Christmas had become a much bigger festival than Easter.

"Ohhhh!" groaned the butterflies, having seen it all before.

"Now what?" asked Darfo, not wanting the Easter Bunny to be punished quite as hard as

Johnny would have liked. Johnny had taken a carrot and was pretending to stuff the bunny with it for dinner.

"Noooo!" Santa said, shaking his head. "We'll do the same as every year…" he indicated to the elves, who picked the bunny up and spun him around and around until he was all dizzy, "…and then I'll fly him to a remote island in the Caribbean… then it takes him a whole year to find his way back here again!"

Butterfly girl Martha raised her hand. Everybody looked at her.

"Ahem!"

"Yes?" said Santa.

"How about if… if… if… we were to let him help us, and then we butterflies could go and help him at Easter?"

Sonya, Darfo and Johnny looked at their friend and the Easter Bunny looked at them all, confused.

"With all that Easter chocolate?" asked Johnny, sharp as a knife.

The Easter Bunny suddenly clicked - he could profit from this: he could make his festival much, much, MUCH bigger than anyone could imagine if he only could win over Santa's legendary butterfly helpers. And everybody in the fairy-tale world knew that they loved sweet stuff.

 "My chocolate is MUCH sweeter than his!" he pointed scornfully at Father Christmas, putting his arms around Johnny and Sonya, who marched towards the toy factory with him in delight. Martha looked at Santa. "That was alright, wasn't it?"

 He gave her a fatherly smile. Poor naïve little thing – she didn't realise what kind of behaviour she was bringing out in them!

 "Ohhhh, sure, of course it's alright, you little Christmas spirit!" he said, thinking to himself, *I wish all families could be more like that at Christmas.*

 Perhaps he would be able to make that into a kind of present!

21

Solstitium - Heliostásion

 The snow fell softly on Santa's Secret City at the North Pole.

At lunchtime, a butterfly girl ran away from her snowball-laden butterfly boyfriend, giggling. The Christmas trees played tripping-up with their roots as they changed places with one another.

The mood was playful and peaceful – it was nearly Christmas.

Then the bell rang – break time was over.

The elves, geese and butterflies chatted away as they wandered back to the present workshops, the Christmas bakery or wherever else they were working today, before getting back to work with gusto. The children of the world – and the odd adult – were going to be delighted! This year, thanks to the butterflies, the Christmas trees and the geese, there would be the best presents ever!

"Ho, ho, ho!" Father Christmas groomed his reindeer Dasher, Dancer, Prancer, Vixen, Comet, Cupid, Donner and Blitzen in joyful anticipation. They were as fit as Christmas fiddles.

He went to take a quick look at Martha, Darfo, Johnny and Sonya's reindeer and was very happy with what he saw. They looked super and were full of energy, racing around in their pens. The butterflies were good reindeer keepers. He was just thinking he must remember to tell them so, when a soft hand reached around and covered up his eyes.

"Ho, ho, ho!" Santa laughed knowingly. Only his wife's hands were that soft!

"No peeping!" she said, binding his eyes with a scarf.

"Now what's happened?"

"Oh, *nothing!*" she whispered in his ear.

"Oh great butterflies, go on, admit it, you're about to ply me with cake to distract me from finding out about some catastrophe or other!"

"Don't always look on the dark side, you old grump!" she said, giving him a slap on the bottom and pushing him forwards.

They waded through snow drifts and then along a path. He had no idea where they were going. He was completely disorientated. Then they brushed past fir trees and snow fell on his cheeks. Santa began to notice that the background noise from the Secret City had changed. The giggles during the whole activity were the same, but the other sounds were different. But they were still in the Secret City, of that he was sure.

"Just a few more steps and we'll be there!" Mrs Claus said, pushing Santa along in front of her. He began to sense the presence of the elves, the butterflies, the geese and the Christmas trees. And he could smell chocolate tea and baked apples. Suddenly it dawned on him!

"Is it… is it… is it that time again?"

Soft violin tones reached his ear. The Elves' Philharmonic was warming up!

"Laa-laa-laa-laaaah!" Martha, Darfo, Sonya and Johnny were practising their songs and the fireflies and the phoenix were blowing candy floss flakes into the air. Then Mrs Claus came to a halt with her husband.

"It's time, isn't it? Go on, admit it, it's time!"

"Well, you know yourself how you forget to look at the calendar every year, what with all the stress!" she said in a gentle voice.

Then somebody lit a big fire. The crackling sound became part of the background noise and the smells completed the bouquet that was in the air.

Mrs Claus undid the scarf and Santa's eyes opened WIDE. All the fairy-tale characters had created a fairground outside in the middle of all the snow.

There were barbecues, dance floors and benches spread about all over the place. Torches lit up the area with their bright flames. The occasional shooting star flew above their heads before taking up its place in the heavens again. St. Peter and Mother Hulda were there too, cuddled up under their cherry blossom blanket.

"You've obviously forgotten that today is December 21st, the winter solstice!"

Which of course meant that there would be a big party up here at the North Pole. Up until now, it had just been the deadline date for the Christmas helpers. If they were on track by now, it meant they were out of the danger zone!

The butterflies had brought in a new Christmas rule which they deemed to be 'extremely, enormously, absolutely, totally important', and without which, they solemnly stated, 'Christmas would be cancelled!!!'

It went thus:

"*Make winter solstice hearty, and party, party, party!*"

22

The Snow Explosion

The snow fell softly on Santa's Secret City at the North Pole. The geese were cackling as they worked hectically and the air was filled with industrious sounds. It was nearly Christmas.

Santa was inspecting all the work stations with a big "Ho, ho, ho!"

The boys were in their workshop making 'presents for men', whilst the girl elves and butterfly girls were shaping, filing and gluing 'the best girls' presents you've ever seen!'

Father Christmas was more than happy. There would be no problems now, the speed that they were working at.

There were two people up above, a level higher than Santa's Secret City, who were happy too. All was going to plan in High Cloud City Palace. The Chief Weather Maker kept aiming his weather machine at different coordinates, and each time, Mother Hulda rushed there on her special cloud and let her snow machine beat out more magic pillows than it had ever done before. Once she was back with St. Peter, she switched off her cloud and hopped off into High Cloud City Palace.

St. Peter was pouring over a pile of maps, contemplating how he was going to distribute the masses of snow upon the world over the next few weeks, when a soft, warm hand covered up his eyes. Then he felt her cheek against his. He stopped working with a smile. He beamed all over his face when she uncovered his eyes as he could see that there was nobody around watching them.

"Hello, you!" she purred to him, pressing her nose to his.

"Hello you!" he whispered back, looking into her eyes, seeing little stars dancing around for what felt like an eternity.

"I don't have much time," she said, first giving him an Eskimo kiss and then a proper one. St. Peter leaned back and accidentally pressed the buttons on his weather machine! The target-finder jumped from here to there, from Africa to Asia, from Europe to America, until it finally fixed on Santa's Secret City. To make matters worse, he had his arm around Mother Hulda and didn't notice that he was squeezing the 'cloud movement' button on the remote control in his hand. The heavenly snow cloud automatically moved to its new position.

It felt like an eternally long kiss, but the eternally long cuddle was losing its squeeze so St. Peter tightened his grip again, this time accidentally switching the snow machine to 'ultra-top-maximum-speed', a setting that had never, ever been used before!

And kissy-kiss-kiss.

To start with, the fairy-tale people a level below them didn't notice a thing. Martha was wearing her snowflake dress and had spent the past ten minutes dreaming about finally holding Darfo in her arms again. It was no good being separated from one another for such a long time, so she decided to take a short break to go and give her sweetheart a kiss.

Most of the girls in the girls' presents workshop felt the same. Nearly all the girl elves had boyfriends who would be wanting to see them. The only annoying thing was the fact that the boys' workshop was right on the other side of Santa's Secret City.

Of course Johnny had also noticed that Darfo was getting more and more impatient, having spent a whole ten minutes away from Martha, and was making more and more little mistakes when he was putting the men's presents together. Particularly noticeable was his apparently mobile workstation. The little rascal had started work next to Johnny, but his feet were somehow moving him magically closer and closer to the door. Then eventually, as boys can't openly admit such things, he got up to 'go outside for a breath of fresh air'.

He got a big surprise, as there stood Santa next to him with a big, cheesy grin. Mrs Claus had been on her own for long enough too.

Two cheesy grins…

"Fresh-air break?"

"Fresh-air break!"

Johnny clapped his hands to his head and groaned, "Uhhh!"

Santa and Darfo opened the door… to a big, white wall of snow!

"Huh???"

111

The white blanket was thirty metres high and the Secret City was paralysed! Santa looked around frantically. *Think! Think!* he urged himself. But the only noise coming from his head was the clanging of alarm bells – Christmas was in danger!!!

Then his thoughts turned back to Mrs Claus. His poor wife!

By this time, Johnny and a firefly boy were standing next to the two 'men'. The Macho Butterfly gave the snow wall a disrespectful kick. Plop. But nothing happened. Not a single flake came down – the mass of snow was as solid as concrete!

"Uh-oh!"

Beads of sweat appeared on Darfo and Santa's foreheads. *Martha! Mrs Claus!*

The elves had been getting closer to the door for their 'fresh-air break' too. Darfo fiddled about with his wings nervously. His little darling must be terrified in this weather as he wasn't there to hold her in his strong, little arms. His little heart raced faster and faster.

The electric blue firefly was close to a state of panic – his girlfriend was over in the girls' workshop. The girls weren't feeling much better. They too had opened their door and were faced with a massive wall of snow, which they had scratted at but couldn't seem to shift at all.

The firefly girl was in a real state and tears trickled down her cheeks. She hadn't had a kiss for over ten minutes – she was close to death, but rather that than life without him!

Only the few single boys and girls like Johnny and Sonya didn't seem to notice how the rays of love coming from the separated couples were getting stronger and stronger. The strongest rays came from the fireflies, but rays could also be seen coming from Darfo, Santa, Martha and all of the boy and girl elves. Their hearts were verily glowing! Golden rays beamed out into the world, getting brighter and brighter. Their chests lit up more and more. The panic-stricken fireflies reached maximum glow first – it felt as though an outside power had taken over their minds and was controlling their bodies.

Whooosh! The firefly boy involuntarily catapulted himself at the wall of snow, burning through it with his glowing heart.

Hissss! He left a little tunnel behind him... and then Santa, to his own surprise, lost control over his body too!

"Oooopsie!"

He waved his arms in the air as his glowing heart dragged his somewhat heavier body along, and he too disappeared into the wall of snow, leaving the shape outstretched arms, legs and a big body in the snow - creating a main tunnel.

Oh my goodness, what's happening to me? thought Santa.

Then Darfo lead the way through the glorious, white tunnel, followed by one elf after the other.

Plop, plop, slither, slide!

Exactly the same thing had happened to the girls at exactly the same time. They didn't know quite what had hit them as they melted their way through the snow towards their sweethearts. Then the happy couples bumped into each other in the middle of the tunnel and hugged each other joyfully.

Big snogs!!!

Only Johnny and a few of the single elves were left behind, astonished. Nothing was impossible-

and here was the proof! Bemused by the happenings, they clambered into the main tunnel to discover a whole new network of tunnels had been created that joined up most every house, cottage and workplace in Santa's Secret City.

 "Phew! At least Christmas isn't in danger!" they all agreed.

 Well, that's how things are in a fairy-tale world. And perhaps in other places too?...

23

The Women's Revolt

 The snow fell softly on Santa's Secret City at the North Pole. The breeze blew gently through needles of the Christmas trees and the first rays of sun shone on the rooftops. A new day, a new adventure! If you watched carefully, you could see the dawn spreading from cottage to cottage, dancing from bed to bed, kissing the Christmas heroes awake. *Good morning, lazy bones!*

Darfo opened his eyes and grinned with delight. There would be more heroic feats to carry out today – it wasn't long until Christmas.

He shook his wings under the bedclothes, swung himself out of bed and waddled towards the breakfast table.

Johnny let out a big *yaaaawn* and then smiled widely in joyful contemplation of the day. Darfo had leapt out of the four-storey bunk bed first, and now he too shuffled towards the breakfast table. They automatically took up their places and gazed at one other.

There was a short pause, three, two, one… then they noticed that something wasn't quite right. But what? They looked under table, but couldn't see anything there. Johnny put his nose under his wings, but it wasn't that either. They looked at one another again, helplessly.

Normally, there was always fresh candy floss on the table and the smell of warm honey wafting through from the kitchen whilst Martha and Sonya served up… Martha and Sonya?

"Huh?"

The two butterfly boys looked around. There was nobody else except them in the room!

Martha und Sonya's beds were empty.

"Huh???"

Darfo shrugged his shoulders.

Johnny got up and felt under Sonya's blanket. The bed was cold - she was long gone!

"Well?"

Darfo could but shrug his shoulders again. He was still only half awake, since he hadn't been served his breakfast.

"Now what do we do?" Johnny asked, as he looked through the window and saw a group of elves and butterflies striding through the snow. They both ran to the door and risked a peek outside. Could it be an alien invasion? Up here in Santa's City? Then they heard the girls chanting outside:

"What makes a man a man, tra-la-lah!"

"When he does everything that he can, tra-la-lah!"

Perplexed, Darfo and Johnny watched as Santa's door opened and he stuck his head out, half asleep.

What was going on?

It… it… it… looked like the women were demonstrating!

Johnny and Darfo dashed past the mob of women. Martha waved happily to Darfo – and promptly got a ticking off from Sonya.

"Not now!" she hissed.

Darfo and Johnny joined Santa and all three of them were clueless. The girl elves, the butterfly girls, Mrs Claus and even a few girl geese were carrying placards claiming '50 percent', 'More rights for fairy-tale women!' and 'Festival of Love – share the joy and share the work!'

Darfo and Johnny gawped at Santa.

"What do they want?" asked Johnny. Ol' Whitebeard scratched his head, but couldn't think of an answer. Nothing had changed recently - everything was the same as usual, wasn't it?

"Well…"

He was just about to say something as Martha, Sonya and Mrs Claus approached them. The girl elves and girl geese carried on chanting and cackling away in the background.

Santa didn't want any of this nonsense going on in his peaceful Secret City.

118

"Oi! What's going on here?" he asked gruffly. He still hadn't had his chocolate tea and breakfast muffins.

Mrs Claus always got up at least an hour earlier to prepare everything. She knew only too well what a bad mood he got in when he was hungry. She also knew that he was prepared to go to any lengths to get his hands on something to eat!

"Father Christmas!" she said, taking a deep breath, "We have noticed that you, Johnny and Darfo are three to a sleigh, compared to only two in Martha and Sonya's case!"

"So?" asked Johnny, all confused.

"Furthermore, we women do almost all the Christmas housework!"

"So what?" said Johnny, taking a brave step forwards.

"We know that without us, you'd be living in a pigsty – and you probably wouldn't even care. But wouldn't you rather continue to have candy floss for breakfast?"

"I can fetch that myself!" Johnny dared to reply.

Sonya looked grimly at her friends.

"Yes, but do you want to spend Christmas with *us*," Sonya pointed at Martha and the other women, "or would you rather spend it on your own and just give *yourself* a present?!"

Oooh, Johnny swallowed hard. That was blackmail!

Darfo had to admit to himself that he hadn't actually raised a finger since the four of them had moved into Butterfly House and he crept behind Santa, ashamed.

"My dear wife, are you trying to threaten that I'll have to spend Christmas alone…" Father Christmas chuntered, not managing to finish because Mrs Claus interrupted him:

"Well you'll have to, if you don't start helping with the Christmas preparations about the house." Santa lifted his hand and pointed at himself, perplexed.

"Who, *meeeee?*"

"Yes, *youuuuu!*"

Stony silence.

Then Darfo and Johnny clambered up onto his shoulder, babbling their thoughts into his ear like a waterfall. War talk.

120

"Babble, babble, babble!"

"…strong men…", *"…Christmas with the boys…
nooo…"*, *"…No kisses for me… oooh…"*, *"…We're not
just carrying the weight on our shoulders though…"*,
*"…All of mankind will have to join in too, equal rights…
sounds good to me…"*, *"…I still want my candy floss and
hot honey…"* - there was no end to it all!

Mrs Claus was just about to interrupt the
discussion when the 'men' appeared to have come
to a decision.

"So that's what we'll do?"

"Yep, that's what we'll do!" the butterfly boys
nodded.

Okay.

With the sweetest smile he could manage without
chocolate tea and muffins, Santa turned to the
'honourable ladies'.

"My sweetest darlings, it gives me great pleasure
to announce…"

"Just a moment!" Mrs Claus said, grabbing a piece
of a paper and a pen. "I want this in writing!"

He looked up at her in surprise and began again.

"My sweetest darlings, it gives me great pleasure
to announce, dear girl elves, Mrs Claus, girl geese

and butterfly girls, that from today onwards, the number of men's presents under the Christmas tree will be proportional to how much effort they put into decorating and doing general Christmas duties!"

There was a short silence… then they all looked at each another and exploded with delight.

"Hurray!" the demonstrators celebrated.

The boys didn't seem to realise that the women had been pretty scared and would actually have settled for less. And Santa hadn't finished yet!

"And that, my dears, applies to all of mankind and not just the fairy-tale world!"

Mrs Claus looked at her husband, enthralled, and gave her notes to one of the girl elves. The girl elf ran straight to the Christmas printing press and had countless copies made, which she would deliver to every man and boy on earth in the last few days before Christmas.

The fairy-tale women had got more than they had hoped for.

Darfo, Johnny and Father Christmas agreed that there was quite a bit of healthy self-interest in their decision and grinned as they watched the ladies celebrating.

Women always seemed to become totally stressed out during the run-up to Christmas and as Santa, Darfo and Johnny knew, this meant they could quite easily end up in the doghouse. But they weren't the only ones to know this - human men were well aware of it too! Yet all it takes to relieve such a situation is a little help and support, don't you think?

After all, Christmas *is* the Festival of Love…

24

Countdown

The snow… had stopped falling softly on the Secret City at the North Pole. The whole place was alive with hectic activity. Tomorrow it would be Christmas. And it looked like everything was going to plan.

As could be expected, the butterflies' pulse rates were increasing by the minute as Christmas drew closer. They were rushing about with bright red faces, eagerly loading their sleighs.

Johnny was loading his sleigh, the 'Turbo Presento', Darfo was loading his, the 'Happy Heavens', Sonya hers, the 'Surprise Rain' and Martha hers, the 'Heart Filler'.

A chain of elves had formed between the workshop storerooms and the transport loading bay. The presents were wrapped in the most wonderful paper in the world. They were carefully passed from hand to hand along the chain, before being squashed into any available spaces. Martha, Darfo, Sonya and Johnny were dashing around nervously with pens and paper, making sure the presents would reach the right children. They checked off the presents against the delivery notes, which had been authorised by Santa himself.

"Mona, Los Angeles, tricycle?"

"Here!" the last-but-one elf in the chain passed the parcel to the elf in the sleigh, who squeezed it amongst the stacks of other presents as best he could.

"Didier, Paris, video game console?"

"Here!"

124

They carried on… and on… and on, until the first sleigh was full, then the second, the third and finally the fourth. And that was only for the first tour of many – the butterflies and Father Christmas had four-hunderfifth-trillion presents to deliver around the world!

"Ho, ho, ho!"

Santa and Mrs Claus dropped by casually with the three electric blue fireflies and the phoenix, who had chosen to stay with them because it was so much calmer than with the Christmas Helpers. They all grinned at the cheery, industrious butterflies.

"Aren't they doing a super job?" said Mrs Claus, resting her head on Santa's shoulder. Santa nodded.

"I think the children will have one of the best Christmases ever, now we have the butterflies' help."

His sleigh had long since been packed. Pure routine!

Then they watched as the elves prepared the pit stop landing zones for when the butterflies came in to fill up with more presents. There was a pit stop box for every sleigh. The Christmas trees provided roofs with their branches to ensure they didn't get snowed in. Bright landing lights protruded from the snow to mark the way.

The elves piled up the supplies of presents between the Christmas trees, which made the fireflies a little nervous – they were piling the presents higher and higher until they reached the very treetops! When the butterflies had delivered their first load of presents, they would race back here at top speed to collect their next load. Once the butterflies had emptied that supply, the elves would send more presents along the chain from the storeroom to be piled up ready for next time.

The fireflies were in the picture, but the phoenix had only just sussed out the procedure and stood there watching with Father Christmas.

Can we help to stack the presents too? their little faces asked. *We're pretty good at flying!*

"Ho, ho, ho!" Santa laughed. "Go on then!"

No sooner had he spoken as they flew past the present-stacking elves, who were wobbling around about twenty metres off the ground, placing one present on top of the next.

126

All of a sudden, *PLOP* Martha fainted with excitement!

Mrs Claus reached into her winter jacket pocket and pulled out a magic rose. She held it under Martha's nose, who opened her eyes in surprise, shook herself and carried on as though nothing had happened.

Then Mrs Claus went over to her husband and gave him a questioning look. He lifted his hands in submission.

"Yes, yes, okay, you were right. You need to be with them as a co-pilot. We all want Christmas to go off without a hitch!"

24 + 1

The Magical Festival of Love

The snow fell softly on Santa's Secret City at the North Pole… and the time had come. Darfo opened his eyes nervously. Johnny and Sonya were already lying there awake. It was still dark, but for the light of the stars. All was quiet outside. None of the butterflies dared to get up first!

A slow, creaking noise scared them all back under the bedclothes… *CREAAAAAK*… but it was only the door!

Father Christmas poked his head into Butterfly House with a big smile. Darfo and Sonya pulled the covers back down to their noses and stared at him.

"Ho, ho, ho!" he laughed and came in. "I didn't scare you, did I?" The little creatures twitched. What? The butterflies? Scared? *Nooooo!*

They leapt from under the covers and bounced down from their four-storey bunk bed.

Mrs Claus gently nudged her husband to one side to let four elves into the room, who paraded in, each carrying something under a red, velvet cloth. Mrs Claus looked over at Martha. She was still lying motionless in bed, fast asleep, arms around her comfort blanket, a grin on her face.

Mrs Claus smiled. It was obvious why she hadn't woken up. Martha had been dreaming about today and how she would be flying around in the sleigh, distributing presents – and had got so excited that she'd fainted in her sleep!

Mrs Claus calmly pulled out her magic rose and held it under Martha's nose. Martha jumped, woke up and looked around.

Darfo smiled at her lovingly and gave her a big kiss on the cheek.

"Is it… is it… is it *time?*"

Father Christmas interrupted.

"My dear butterflies!" he boomed out in a wise voice, causing Sonya, Darfo and Johnny to stand to attention and stick their little chests out. Their heads were in such a spin that they couldn't manage to say a thing. Martha scrambled out of bed and hurried to join them.

Father Christmas continued, the four elves by his side bearing the gifts.

"My dear butterflies… never before have butterflies managed to enrich the run up to Christmas quite as much as you have this year!"

They all gulped.

"The special glow during the run up to Christmas is produced by those with pure hearts."

Darfo, Sonja, Martha and Johnny's eyes got bigger and bigger.

"And you are about to take your pure hearts around the world to spread feelings of warmth, hope, truth and joy, solidarity, trust and honesty. You will show mankind that the true path lies in charity, consideration, selflessness and a joy for life – and that's what makes the Festival of Love what it is!"

Martha took this as a signal to turn round and give Darfo a big kiss on the cheek. She couldn't help herself!

"Fly out across the world today and convey this to the people, convey it to the children: the future is in their hands!"

The elves took a few steps forwards, one taking place in front of each butterfly.

"It gives me great honour to be able to present you with something that has never been possible before!"

Martha began to feel giddy. Mrs Claus was standing behind her and wafted her magic rose under Martha's nose. *Ahhh! Much better.*

"Now, let's see you in your official Christmas Butterfly clothes!"

This was the signal to the elves. They lifted the velvet cloths, and there lay red trousers, black boots, red Santa-style bobble hats, red coats and black belts with big buckles! Mrs Claus waved the rose around Martha frantically but ended up having to use two roses. The butterflies, speechless and motionless, let the elves dress them in their new outfits. Their arms, legs and wings moved robotically… soon they were dressed just like Father Christmas, but for their wings peeping out of extra slits at the back! The colours of their wings became much more intense as the little rascals glowed with pride.

The elves tweaked the uniforms here and there and then packed their things together and took a few steps back.

Darfo became aware of his surroundings for a very short moment and noticed the geese, the fireflies and the phoenix pressing their faces against the window pane, their mouths and eyes wide open. Elves squeezed in between them and the Christmas trees joined in with a few branches.

Even Mother Hulda and St. Peter had used their ten-minute tea break to come and see the ceremony.

Father Christmas cleared his throat.

"Well, my dear butterflies," he boomed, making the little rascals jump. "The time has come!"

His white beard began to sizzle and crackle with magic. Darfo and Johnny's bobble hats slipped over their eyes and they pushed them back up subconsciously.

Gold-glowing crystals sparked out of Santa's chest. They were the same colour as the magic, golden rings that were now leaping from Santa's boots and shooting up his legs. The wind blew the door open a little further and four shooting stars whizzed in out of the darkness, dancing gaily about Butterfly House.

"Now it's time for you to become part of the Christmas magic!" Santa spoke in a deep, caring voice as he walked up to Darfo.

The golden crystals poured over Darfo, enveloping him in a milky haze. Two of the shooting stars crashed into one other above

Santa's Little Helper and star dust rained down on him.

Father Christmas lifted his index finger and pointed it through the haze at Darfo's heart. The magic golden rings joined together and raced down Santa's arm straight into Darfo's heart, before returning to Santa, where they spun wildly around his body, *PLING!*

Darfo suddenly felt very calm and collected. His golden heart beat in his chest and he felt much more himself again.

"Hee, hee, hee, hee!" he giggled, scratching himself.

Then Santa turned to Johnny.

The golden crystals covered him in a haze, two shooting stars crashed together again, the star dust fell on him and Father Christmas gave him that final touch, *PLING!*

Santa continued immediately, turning to Sonya, giving the butterfly lady her Christmas magic, *PLING!*

Despite the fact that Martha now had five magic roses waving under her nose, she still only experienced all this in a kind of trance. But the

crystals still covered her in a haze, shooting stars
gave her dust and Santa pointed at her too,
PLING!

The effect was visible right away - she came back
to life again, giving herself a shake.

It was done!

The shooting stars shot back into the sky and
Santa's magic vanished from sight with a hiss.

"Hurray!" the mini-Santas celebrated, hugging one
another.

Everybody in the room ran to shake hands with
them, congratulate them and give them a very
quick cuddle – they didn't have much time!

"Ho, ho, ho!"

Santa, who looked his usual self again by now,
pointed outside. The reindeer's bells signalled that
the elves had Santa's sleigh and the butterflies' four
sleighs at the ready. The reindeer waited proudly,
fidgeting nervously with their hooves. It was time
to go!

It took a while for everybody to wish them well.
Then the butterflies marched behind Father
Christmas to their flying Christmas transporters.

"Are you coming with me?" Martha whispered to Mrs Claus, who nodded gently.

"I sure am!"

Martha smiled.

Brightly coloured piles of presents filled the sleighs. The lists for the first tour were ready. The Christmas butterflies took up their places, deep in thought.

An electric blue firefly joined each of the other butterflies and the phoenix sat next to Santa, glowing. Santa looked at him in surprise and the phoenix gave him a cheeky grin as if to say, *Of course I'm here – I wasn't going to stay behind on my own!* Santa looked to the front and nodded once.

"Ho, ho, ho!" Father Christmas called, taking the reins in his hands.

"Ho, ho, ho!" called Martha, Darfo, Sonya and Johnny, picking up their reins too and pressing their magic hover buttons.

Five glittery sleighs lifted into the air with their drivers, all dressed in their red suits with their red bobble hats, fully laden and ready to go.

"Ho, ho, ho!" they all called.

The elves, the geese, the Christmas trees, the fireflies and the phoenix, St. Peter, Mother Hulda, the butterflies, Santa and Mrs Claus, everybody waved as they prepared to set off.

"Ho, ho, ho!" they shook their reins.

Everybody applauded, *clap, clap, clap, clap, clap!*

The Reindeer started to trot… and then shot up into the snowy Christmas sky.

The time had come, "HO, HO, HO!!!"

Because…

When seconds become hours and then turn back to seconds, you can be sure it's Christmas time:

PRESENT TIME!

Printed in Poland
by Amazon Fulfillment
Poland Sp. z o.o., Wrocław